DIAMONDBACK McCALL And the City Beneath the Sand

DIAMONDBACK McCALL And the City Beneath the Sand

•

Robert Middleton

AVALON BOOKS
NEW YORK

Library of Congress Catalog Card Number: 2005901086
ISBN 0-8034-9741-5

Published by Thomas Bouregy & Co., Inc.
160 Madison Avenue, New York, NY 10016

PRINTED IN THE UNITED STATES OF AMERICA
ON ACID-FREE PAPER
BY HADDON CRAFTSMEN, BLOOMSBURG, PENNSYLVANIA

To my lovely wife, Denise, whose support
and encouragement are responsible
for this book's completion.

For their thoughtful comments and suggestions,
my sincere thanks to the following special people:

Larry Channey
Carol Biller
Rick Ciauri
Rita and Larry Bittner
Skip Middleton

Chapter One
Diamondback McCall

If you looked to the top of the front page of the day's local newspaper, it read: THE TUCSON DAILY STAR, April 29, 1884. Turn to page three, and there was an article on John Burrow's Western Carnival. The article announced that there would be one performance of the traveling show that afternoon in Tucson.

There were the usual acts: a lady bareback rider, a cowboy doing rope tricks, and lots of Indians. But the star of the show, the one everyone came to see, was Jack "Diamondback" McCall. He was famous for being a dead shot with a rifle, six-gun, or even a knife. Jack was also known for the flashy rope and riding tricks he did aboard his palomino stallion, Chilco. However, what people really came to see, or a least try to see, was the absolute fastest gun ever on earth! So fast that if you saw anything at all, it was simply a blur.

Years earlier, someone pinned Diamondback to his name, suggesting Jack's speed was like that of the well-known rattlesnake. The truth of the matter was, compared to Jack McCall, a rattlesnake wasn't all that fast. Still, the name stuck.

What the article didn't mention was that this was Jack's last performance. John Burrow had known for months that Tucson would be Jack's last show. He had spent that time, without success, trying to convince him to stay. But Jack had other plans. In the next town the show would have a new shooter, Pistol Pete Dodd. He would join them in Phoenix. Dodd was quite a marksman in his own right. He was also very fast, just not as fast as Diamondback McCall. Of course, no one was. Nevertheless, as they say, the show would go on.

The show in Tucson went on as usual with Jack at his typical perfection. It was held at the Tucson rodeo grounds. It ended a little past 6:00P.M. The cast then met back at their hotel in town for a little farewell for Jack. He, on the other hand, never cared much for goodbyes. So Jack met with them quickly and then went upstairs to his room. He changed into what he called his city slicker clothes and then headed for the Longhorn Saloon, just down the street.

Jack had learned that the only way for him to move about undisturbed in public was for people not to recognize him. Wearing the city duds usually worked. The black felt bowler covered his wavy black hair. The half-length gray tweed coat hid not only his powerful build, but more importantly, his two pearl-handled Colt .45s. They resided in low slung black holsters, the initials JDM prominent on each one in silver lettering. There was, quite obviously, no disguising his six-foot height, rugged good looks, or steel gray eyes.

Chapter Two
Friends and Foes

Tucson was growing faster since the railroad reached it four years earlier. But in many ways, it was a typical cow town. It was turning dusk as Jack walked the rutted street with cowpokes ambling by. The Longhorn's lively mixture of voices and music found its way into the street. The dimming sunlight made the saloon's red paintwork turn to a brownish color. It was two stories high with windows on both floors. If it was like most saloons, there were rooms up there to rent by the night or by the hour. A longhorn skull hung appropriately above the words LONGHORN SALOON, high above the swinging doors.

Jack paused before the swinging doors. A tangled scent of kerosene, booze, and tobacco smoke flowed by the doorway. The pungent but familiar smell of all saloons. There were kerosene lamps resting on wagon wheels supported by chains from the ceiling and others on the walls. He walked in and looked around. In the large open space before the L-shaped bar there were scattered tables, all in use, for gambling and drinking. Back in the far left corner by the stairs was a thin man playing an out of tune upright piano as a saloon girl sang "Clementine".

There were other girls pushing drinks and other commodities. Behind the bar was all dark wood and mirrors. Bottles and glasses were stacked on shelves below the mirrors.

There was a beer tap attached to the bar itself, which was made of red oak. On the right end, the bar made a turn back to the wall forming an L. That portion of the bar was about half the length of the main bar. It had a flip-up top that the barmaids used to pass through.

There was an older man halfway down that L-shaped portion of the bar. He was trying to tell a young cowpoke about when he was a deputy sheriff. The cowpoke wouldn't listen though, and even seemed to enjoy making fun of him. Jack studied the old man for a few moments. He was maybe five-feet-eight and just a little chubby. He wore his off-white Stetson way back on his head, in a friendly sort of way. Somewhere along the line, a pair of tan suspenders replaced a gun-belt. His gray hair and beard, weathered round face, and well-worn white shirt and denim pants all spoke of experience. Jack thought it odd how so many people dismissed another man's experience.

The young cowpoke left the old-timer's side to mosey over toward a card table. Jack took his spot at the bar and glanced to his right at the old man and smiled. The old man smiled right back, adding, "Howdy, you're new in town." He said it flatly with a harsh woodsy twang.

"You don't miss much. Do you?" Jack offered his hand. "The name's Jack."

The old man clasped Jack's hand eagerly and returned, "Dakota Dan Smith, but forget the Smith part. And I guess I do notice the comings and goings of folks more than most."

Jack noticed Dakota Dan's beer mug was empty and asked the bartender for a couple brews. The heavy man had a black waxed mustache, thick wavy hair and wore a stained white apron that seemed to reach his shoes. He efficiently filled two mugs from the tap and slid them to where the bar made the turn. Jack then pulled them in front of himself and a grateful Dakota Dan.

They each took a swig, then Jack turned to his new friend, "Did I hear you say you used to be a deputy sheriff?"

"Yup, almost ten years of it."

"That must be why you tend to notice people."

"Sure, got to be a habit with me. Sometimes it's

little things." Dan leaned forward and looked down the long bar. "Sometimes it's real plain like right there." He motioned toward the five men standing at the front bar. "Now forget about the two cowboys nearest to us. But you see the three galutes in the middle of the bar?"

Jack gave a nod.

"Well, they're a mean bunch on a good day. Hired guns from the Triple B Ranch. But see the tall man in the middle?"

"Yeah, wearing the new Stetson?" Jack replied.

"Yup, and that ain't all that's new. Along with that hat, he's wearing new boots and britches. All black to go along with the rest of his duds."

Jack looked puzzled, "Is that all?"

"Nope, he's Curly McBride, and he's been buying drinks for lots of folks and throwing money around for a couple hours now. And I happen to know that the Triple B Ranch doesn't pay their men for a couple more days."

"And like most ranches, the Triple B Ranch pays once a month."

"Yup. Ever heard of a cowhand or hired gun that had much money at the end of the month?"

Jack gave the suspect a careful look and shook his head. "Mighty interesting, Dan."

They spent the next half-hour downing a couple more beers and wondering what McBride had been up to. The three men from the Triple B were now the only ones left on the front side of the bar. They had been loud and rowdy at times and the other two cowboys went elsewhere.

Jack and Dan were still sipping their beer at the side bar when an Indian came through the swinging doors. He was rather thin and about medium height. His clothes were all of an alabaster-colored cotton. The pants were a little on the short side. His shirt fit loosely and was decorated with beads of turquoise along the front. Atop his long black hair was a single hawk's feather. Jack noticed that he looked quite pale.

Dan shook his head. "They don't allow Indians in saloons around here. And he sure looks like he could use a drink."

Jack felt concern for the Indian, he looked nervous and so pale. The Indian seemed to focus on McBride at the bar and then slowly walked up behind him. "We make deal." He spoke to McBride's back.

McBride had seen the Indian come in and walk up to him in the mirror above the bar but ignored him.

"We make deal," he said louder. "You take money, no buy medicine!"

McBride slowly turned around. He had the hard chiseled features of a killer and cold dark eyes. The tall man stared down at the Indian. "You looking for trouble, Injun? You know you ain't allowed in here!"

While this was taking place, Jack leaned closer to Dan. "Is anyone in here likely to stop this before it gets out of hand?"

Dakota turned to Jack's ear. "See how McBride's friends are moving apart?" Indeed, the shorter, stouter man dressed in buckskin with the tan Stetson had moved almost to the far wall. The thinner, rangier one dressed almost completely in gray had moved to the edge of the bar near Jack and Dan. Dakota spoke softly, "McBride has got his men covering him in a crossfire. A man would have to be crazy to step in there. And they're all fast with a shootin' iron, especially McBride." Dan just shook his head solemnly.

"You take money! We make deal!" the Indian pleaded and apparently wasn't going to back down.

They could see the anger building in McBride's face. "I don't make deals with Injuns. Now you've got one minute to get out of here or I'm gonna make you a good Injun."

McBride had plainly eluded to an old saying that Jack cared little for: "A good Indian is a dead Indian." It came about during the Indian wars and, indeed, some tribes made for ruthless enemies. Jack's experience, in contrast, had found them to be men of honor.

It was now obvious that something had to be done. This had gone far enough. Jack turned and walked toward the Indian. Dan had been so engrossed in the drama unfolding that he hadn't noticed Jack leaving his side. He felt a sickness in his stomach when he saw where Jack was heading.

Jack stepped right between the Indian and McBride, taking McBride by surprise. He then turned to the Indian, face-to-face. "Let me take care of this," Jack said sincerely.

The Indian was very scared and pointed at McBride and said, "He take money. No buy medicine."

Jack nodded and put both hands on his shoulders. "You can trust me."

The Indian looked hard into Jack's eyes and returned a nod, "I think maybe I can."

"Wait outside while I sort this out." Jack said calmly.

The Indian followed Jack's request while Jack turned to face Curly McBride.

McBride stood there impatiently and looking as mean and angry as before. "Well, that was real sweet, greenhorn, but I didn't need any help getting rid of that Injun. He might have gone out feet first, but he'd have been gone just the same." He gave a quick laugh. "And I don't take kindly to some dude sticking his nose in my business!"

Jack looked straight into McBride's cold eyes. "Well, Curly, you don't mind me calling you

Curly? The Indian may be gone, but you've still got to deal with me."

McBride looked puzzled. "I don't know what you're talking about, greenhorn!"

For effect, Jack made a point of using McBride's first name. Each time he'd say it, you could hear his contempt for the man. "You see, Curly, the Indian says you owe him money, and I believe him."

Dakota Dan put his hands over his eyes, shaking his head, afraid to watch. The bartender moved quickly over by Dakota and then ducked behind the bar. Throughout the rest of the saloon, everyone else was moving out of the line of fire and watching intensely.

"Nobody accuses me of being a thief, especially some dude!"

"Just pay back the money, and I won't have to hurt you." Jack stated matter-of-factly.

McBride looked up and down at Jack in his city slicker suit and burst into laughter. He looked each way at his two amigos, spurting out through the laughter. "You hear that, boys? He doesn't want to hurt me!" They chuckled with him.

Jack glanced at McBride's two gun-hands. "Friends of yours?"

The laughter petered out. "That's right, friends of mine." He sounded like he was tired of the banter.

"Well, bring them on in, I want to meet all your friends." There was sarcasm in the tone.

McBride glanced around the room at his audience. "Yeah, why not?" He then made little gestures with two tilts of the head and they quickly joined him at each side. The trio were quite serious now. McBride's words came with finality. "Well dude, like you wanted," he gestured to his right and left, "meet Les and Cord. But you ain't gonna know them for long. Not where you're going!"

"Well, it's this way. I think you should at least know a man's name before you kill him."

"That's it dude! You ain't funny no more. But," he shook his head, "you've got brass!"

Jack used the forefingers of each hand to gently slip his tweed jacket behind the pearl handles of his two revolvers. "I've got lead too." He smiled. "Enough for all of you."

For the first time, perhaps in his entire life, McBride's cold eyes showed some fear. His voice went higher. "Mister, you got a name?"

"Jack McCall," he answered flatly.

Cord was tilting his head so he could read the initials on Jack's holster. "So what's the D stand for?" He posed the question softly to his amigos.

Les stared at the weapons strapped low to Jack's waist. His words came out with a waver. "There's only one man who carries iron like that." He turned and gave Cord an uneasy glance. "Diamondback McCall."

"Diamondback McCall!" The name got stuck in Cord's throat and came out in a yelp.

All three men seemed to deteriorate before everyone's eyes. Cord was so nervous that he tried to talk, but couldn't. McBride seemed to handle the shock best. He gathered himself. "You as fast as they say, McCall?" There was a quiver in his voice.

Jack grinned. "I was hoping you were a curious man. Now you know how to find out, don't you?" Jack paused. "Whenever you're ready, boys, make your play." He focused on the three men. Of course he knew he could easily outdraw them. But Jack could read a man's eyes and he knew that these men were too scared to draw. He also knew that these men were bullies at best and usually far worse. They deserved to know how it felt to be bullied and humbled.

The three of them momentarily glanced at each other and seemed to raise their hands away from their guns and shake their heads in unison. McBride blurted, "Now, now, easy there Mr. McCall. We're not looking for trouble from the likes of you. We'll just find us another saloon." He even managed a little consoling smile.

The three started to turn and move toward the door. But Jack held a Colt .45 in his right hand about six inches from McBride's nose. They never saw him take it from his holster, it just suddenly appeared. McBride blinked in bewilderment.

"It's not that easy, boys." Jack twirled the pistol and spun it back into the holster. "Put your holsters on the bar, boys." He stated firmly.

They looked at each other and then grudgingly complied.

"Good." Jack spoke softer. "Now, Curly, how much money did you get from the Indian? And remember he's just outside."

"Thirty dollars," answered a beaten McBride.

"That's a lot of money. How much do you have left?"

"None, I spent it all."

"In one day! Well, you know what they say about a fool and money."

Chuckles went through the room.

"Well, I guess we'll just have to keep the gun as partial payment, but somehow I don't think it's the only one you own." Jack glanced at McBride's partners. "You two can collect your guns tomorrow afternoon, but you're heading back to the ranch tonight."

They nodded. Then all three started to leave.

Jack held up his left hand. "I said Les and Cord could go, not you, Curly."

Les and Cord quickly dashed out through the swinging doors.

"We're not quite even." Jack gave McBride a glare and shook his head.

McBride looked back at Jack and shrugged his shoulders. "I told you I spent the money."

"Well," Jack looked McBride up and down. "Looks to me like you bought some new duds today."

He nodded.

"Put the hat on the bar."

He did.

Jack looked down at McBride's boots. "Put the boots on the bar." Chuckles went around the room again. McBride gave a little grimace and then pulled them off and placed them by the hat. Jack was still looking down. "Those look like new britches."

McBride shook his head. "That's going too far, McCall," he stated defiantly.

Jack stared at him coldly. "It's your choice, Curly. Take off the pants or put on the holster!"

McBride dropped his head dejectedly and started unbuttoning his trousers. The room was filled with laughter. McBride left his pants on the bar and made his way out of the saloon. Somehow, as everyone saw him in his faded red long johns, he didn't look so tough.

Chapter Three
Brad Barlow

The saloon quickly settled back to its normal routine with most everyone going back to the tables and bar. Although many eyes and much conversation would be on Jack that night, the drama was clearly over.

Jack walked back to Dakota Dan. Dan turned and shook Jack's hand with enthusiasm. "That was sure something to see," he said with a grin. "When you first went over there, I thought you were a goner. Of course, I didn't know who you were, then."

"I'm glad you found it interesting, Dan."

"Oh, it was mighty interesting."

Jack motioned toward the swinging doors. "I wonder if you'd mind asking my Indian friend to come in while I talk to the barkeep?"

"You bet, partner."

Jack got the bartender's attention and the big man hurried over. "I'll be taking McBride's things with me," he informed him. "Maybe you could hang on to his pals' hardware until they come after them."

"I'll do just that, Mr. McCall," he answered with a big smile.

"Much obliged," responded Jack as he turned to go to Dan and the Indian, who were talking near the entrance.

Jack felt the bartender's hand on his shoulder and turned back to him.

"Mr. McCall, sir. Do you have a place to stay tonight?"

"The Benton Hotel. Why?"

"Well, sir, I was hoping I could convince you to stay here. We have rooms upstairs that are bigger and I think nicer than the Benton's. And there would be no charge."

Jack shook is head. "What's this all about?"

"Well, I know a bit about the saloon business, Mr. McCall. Because of what you did tonight, this place will draw cowboys from all over. But lately, my rooms have been mostly empty. If they knew Diamondback McCall stayed here, I think that would change."

Jack couldn't imagine anyone staying in one of the rooms upstairs just because he had, but he considered the bartender's proposal. "You have anything against Indians staying here?"

He shook his head nervously, "Oh, no, Mister McCall. Any friend of yours is welcome here."

"I'm thinking the Benton probably isn't as open-minded as you are. Guess I'll take you up on your offer." He gave the bartender a nod of thanks. The big man returned a smile.

Jack looked over at the Indian and studied him for a moment. He not only looked pale, but Jack wondered how long it had been since he had anything to eat. "Any chance of getting some food here?"

"Sure thing, Mr. McCall. We bring dinners in from a café down the street all the time."

"Good, we'll be at the table in the corner behind the piano. Three of us." Jack smiled. "Thank you kindly."

He picked up McBride's things and then met Dan and the Indian midway across the room and led them to the corner table. Jack took the chair with the back against the wall, looking toward the swinging doors. The gunfighter's seat. Dan and the Indian sat to his right and left.

Just then the bartender arrived with three beers. "On the house, of course. And I sent a girl for the food. It'll be here soon. Can I get you anything else?" he asked still smiling.

Jack shook his head. Dan's eyes followed the bartender's exit then went back to Jack. "Funny thing, I don't think I ever saw that man so happy before. Anyway, your Indian friend here, Chota, was just telling me that McBride overheard him trying to buy some medicine for his people. Of course, the sad truth is, a lot of places around here won't sell to Indians. Anyway, McBride took his money and said he'd buy it for him."

"And we know the rest," Jack responded. "So, tomorrow, we'll go sell McBride's things and then see about Chota's medicine."

"You good man, Mr. McCall." Chota still looked pale but at least he now wore a smile.

"It's just Jack, Chota." He turned to Dan. "How long do you figure before our friend McBride decides to try something?"

"You read him right. My guess is he needs a little time to plan something lowdown and sneaky, like a back-shootin'." Dan paused and thought a bit. "But when a man like McBride loses the respect of the other men at that ranch, or Barlow himself, he might do almost anything."

"Barlow's the owner?"

"Yup. A rich but no-good fancy-Dan from back east."

"Where's he from?"

"Nobody knows. He just showed up here a few years ago with a lot of money. First he bought the old Svenson spread. Then, with the help of

McBride and his pals, started grabbing up all the small ranches around him. You know, sell or die."

"So he steals what people have put their whole lives into. Nice man. He probably cries all the way to the bank."

"Yup, except he don't trust banks. It's a quirk of his. Even his cowhands think it's funny. Seems he has a big safe in his house. He's the only one that knows the combination and he's got two men guarding it round the clock."

Jack smiled, "Maybe McBride will end up doing permanent safe guard duty." Dan gave a quick laugh.

Just then the bartender, with a saloon girl in tow, arrived with dinner. They placed big steaks with beans, potatoes, and lots of bread and butter before them. The bartender sent the girl for more beer and then looked at Jack. "Mr. McCall, Room One is all ready for you with two beds."

Jack's eyes moved to Dan who was busy carving his steak. "You think we ought to stick together to-night with McBride on the loose?"

Dan spoke between chewing. "Might not be a bad idea to watch each other's back."

Jack turned back to the bartender. "Can you move a third bed into that room for my friend here?" he motioned toward Dan.

"I'll see to it Mr. McCall."

As the bartender left the trio to enjoy their din-ner, Dan's eyes moved to catch Jack's attention. His face wore an uneasy look. "How long you figure on staying in town?"

"Just until morning."

"That's what I thought." His eyes seemed to squint a little as he went on. "Would you mind me riding along? There ain't nothin' or nobody holdin' me here."

"Wouldn't have it any other way."

A boyish grin spread across Dakota Dan's face and a glint could be seen in his eyes.

After they finished the meal, Dan grabbed McBride's things, and Chota followed him upstairs to the room. Jack had to go back to the Benton Hotel to pick up his saddlebags, bedroll, and Winchester rifle.

He checked out of the room and then headed back to the Longhorn. By the time he had joined Dan and Chota in the room, they were both in bed and Dan was already asleep. Jack was amused by how Dan was watching his back. He set the saddlebags, bedroll, rifle, and his hat on the dresser by the door and then laid on his bed. He stayed dressed, armed, and ready to move quickly. He would sleep lightly that night.

The sun had been up less than an hour before Jack got up. The night had passed slowly with every little noise causing him to open his eyes and become alert again. He wasn't fully rested but he felt good.

Jack took his riding clothes from his saddlebags. They were the clothes that he wore in the show, the clothes that people were used to seeing him in. After what happened last night, there was little point in trying to go unnoticed. The pants, shirt, vest, and hat were basic black. What made the outfit unique was the snakeskin boots, belt, and hatband. He dressed and then began the routine of washing and shaving at a table with a mirror. A pitcher of water and a bowl had been provided.

He finished without waking his two friends but then there were loud voices from downstairs. He also heard a commotion from outside in the street. The sounds caused Dan and Chota to wake with a start. They jumped from their beds and followed Jack to a window overlooking the front of the saloon for a look-see. There were nearly twenty men on horseback in front of the saloon.

Dan rubbed his eyes, took a gander, and then shook his head. "This is big trouble, partner! Those are the men from the Triple B and that's Brad Barlow up front on that gray appaloosa."

Barlow looked to be average height but stocky. He had a wide flat face with a black mustache below a prominent nose. He wore expensive-looking tan riding clothes, but no gun.

Jack nodded, "And there's our three friends from last night right behind that big fellow on the big bay." He smiled. "What a surprise."

"That big hombre is Butch Cole," Dan added, "the ranch foreman."

Jack observed the situation. Barlow was at the very front. Butch Cole was right behind him. McBride, Cord, and Les were behind the foreman, with the rest of the men fanned out in the back. One of the men in the back, on the left side, was holding the reins of a riderless pinto. All of those men's attention seemed to be on the shouting that was going on inside the saloon, which was getting louder.

Jack turned away from the window and looked around the room. Beside Dan's bed were McBride's things, along with Dan's hat and boots. He went over and pulled McBride's gun from the holster. Then he spun the cylinder, noted it was loaded, and slipped it in his belt, by the buckle. There were a lot of guns down in the street. An extra pistol seemed like a good idea. As he headed for the door, he stopped at the dresser and picked up his hat.

"What are you gonna do, Jack?" Dan queried.

"I've got to go sort this out," he answered and then left the room.

Dan looked down and counted eighteen men waiting in the street and then looked at Chota. "That's gonna take a heap of sortin'."

Chota nodded.

Jack stood just beyond the door of the room.

While he listened to the voices downstairs, he practiced his draw. Just like the moments before a show, he'd pull the pistols out of the holsters faster and faster until he was ready. During that time, he could hear what was going on. One of the men from the Triple B was trying to get the bartender to tell him where Diamondback McCall was. To his credit, the bartender wasn't talking.

Jack walked down the stairs. There was a young gun-hand facing the bartender with his back to the stairs. He was wearing dusty leather chaps, a faded white shirt and wore his gun like he knew how to use it. The bartender just stood there, near the far corner of the bar, nervously shaking his head while the gunman threatened him. But the gun-hand was yelling so loud that he didn't hear Jack come up behind him. It wasn't until he saw the bartender's eyes move toward Jack, that he turned toward him. The man went for his gun, but before he even touched it, the barrel of Jack's .45 was against his nose.

"The name's McCall," he stated coldly. "You wanted me?" He twirled the gun and then sank it into the holster.

The young man, caught off guard, just stood there.

"Well, what do you want, sonny?"

The man's eyes were still blinking and his words

seemed to stumble out. "It's, it's Mr. Barlow that wants to see you sir. He's outside waiting."

"Alright, sonny. Tell your boss to just keep waiting out in the street. I'll be coming out in a few minutes."

"Mr. Barlow's not used to people telling him what to do."

"Tell him to get used to it. And tell him what I said, sonny, word for word. Now, before you go, I want you to remember that the bartender here is a personal friend of mine. You bother him again and I won't like it! So, once you hand over your holster, you can go." Jack put his left hand out, palm up.

The young man balked. There was pride in his eyes.

"I'm doing you a favor, sonny. If you don't have a gun, I won't have to kill you."

The gunman showed some displeasure before he grudgingly complied. Jack then tossed the holster onto the bar. But anger consumed the young man as he headed for the swinging doors. "This ain't gonna change anything, McCall," he blurted as he turned back toward Jack. "There are still another eighteen men outside with guns. Those are poor odds!"

Jack smiled, "Yeah, you should have brought more men."

The young gun hesitated, giving Jack a long, perplexed expression. He then quickly turned and bolted through the swinging doors. While the gun-hand went out to convey Jack's message, the bartender told Jack what he knew. It seemed that there was a cowboy in the saloon the previous night that had overheard part of their conversation about where Jack would be staying. Cowboys like to talk, and that information ended up known to the Triple B boys. Jack thanked him for his discretion and peered out the front window. By now, Barlow was chastising his gun-hand who, shortly thereafter, went back to his waiting pinto.

Jack McCall got no pleasure from telling people off or pushing them around. What he had done in dealing with the gun-hand and Barlow was simply tactical. From what Dan had told him, he knew a lot about the man. He was rich, powerful, and used to getting his own way. He also seemed arrogant and impatient. Jack wanted to use this against him to narrow the odds. This was a man that liked to talk big but wore no gun. He took no risks. He had his own personal little army to back up his words. Jack knew if he kept him waiting long enough, Barlow's temper would get the better of him, and he could see it building in his face.

Somehow, he knew the time was right and he stepped in front of the swinging doors and leaned on them. He looked straight at Barlow. "I thought I finished with you Triple B boys last night."

For a moment Barlow simply returned a cold,

hard stare. When that only produced a smile on Jack's face, he gritted his teeth and nudged his horse forward. There were hitching rails on both sides of the saloon's entrance. Barlow rode to the one on Jack's left, jumped off, and threw the reins around the rail. Jack passed through the swinging doors as Barlow walked toward him.

"Nobody keeps me waiting!" Barlow bellowed. "And nobody insults my men. When you insult them, you insult me!"

They were almost together by then. Barlow started to say the word "You", but as he opened his mouth, Jack drew both guns. As usual, no one actually saw him make the move; both Colt .45s just suddenly appeared. One was pointed right at the foreman, Butch Cole, the other gun was inside Barlow's mouth. Jack walked forward, forcing Barlow up against the hitching rail, and startling his horse.

Jack looked at the foreman, "Mr. Cole, if any one of your men go for their guns, you'll be the second dead man. Right behind your boss here!" He punctuated the last statement with the click, click sound of the gun in Barlow's mouth being cocked. Barlow was whimpering and having a little trouble breathing, but Jack kept his eyes on the foreman and company.

Cole motioned with his hand to back off and turned to his men. "Nobody goes for their gun, not yet anyway!" He sounded like he was in control, but some of his men had other ideas. McBride uttered, "He's only one man."

Then Les added, "How can we let him face-down the whole dang ranch?"

"Yeah, nobody can take eighteen guns." Cord stated firmly.

"Maybe not, but he could kill ten or twelve of us!" The foreman ended the debate.

Jack scanned his rivals. "I want you boys to think about something. Who's going to open that big safe and pay you if I happen to squeeze this trigger? Who else knows the combination to that safe?"

Rumblings went through the men. Butch Cole nodded and looked at Jack. "You know we haven't been paid in quite a while. But you also gotta know we can't just leave the boss this way."

Jack gave a quick smile. "Oh, you don't have to worry about that, Butch. Mr. Barlow came into town today just to talk to me. Isn't that right, Brad?" Jack tilted the barrel of the .45 in Barlow's mouth up and down, making it look like Barlow was nodding in agreement. "And you'd like these boys of yours to go back to the ranch so we can have a nice friendly talk, right?" Again, he used the gun barrel to make Barlow nod his head. "Well, Butch, sounds like you've got your orders."

The foreman paused, reached up with the fore-finger of his right hand, and tilted back his hat. He then just sat there for a few seconds and scratched his head. After what seemed like a very long moment, he finally turned to his men. "Alright, boys, you heard the boss, we're riding back to the ranch."

Most of the men, happy to have found a way out of the showdown, rode out at a full gallop. McBride and his two pals stayed and glared at Jack briefly in mock defiance, and then rode off.

Dan then came through the swinging doors carrying Jack's Winchester rifle. "I thought I was going to have to try and figure out this fancy long gun on Barlow's boys. I sure was glad you didn't need me. I never shot one before."

Jack pulled his pistol from Barlow's mouth and then spun both .45s back into their holsters. "It's good to know you're there to back me up, Dan." He took Curly's pistol from his belt and offered it to him. "Why don't you hang on to this one for a while, instead?"

Dan still had the Winchester in his right hand, so he took the pistol from Jack with his left hand, and handed him the rifle. He then looked at the six-shooter and then up at his friend. "Eighteen men and eighteen bullets. That was cutting it a little fine, wasn't it, partner?"

Jack smiled, "Maybe, but was it interesting?"

A big grin appeared on Dan's face. "Mighty!"

Chota then came out and joined his amigos. He

looked at Barlow and couldn't hold back a wry smile. "Big man wet pants."

By this time people were gathering. The bartender, a girl from the saloon and several locals came to see Barlow in his embarrassing condition. They could not help but giggle a little. It was easy to see that Barlow was angry, and quite apparent that he was still too scared to even talk.

Jack looked down at Barlow's accident and tried not to smile. "You didn't really have anything to say to me, did you, Mr. Barlow?"

He just shook his head.

"Good. Then we'll just send you on your way."

Barlow looked surprised and relieved.

"But, leave the pants and boots here, they're really soaked. I'm sure, with you being so well-liked and respected around here, we'll find someone to wash them for you."

Barlow shook his head with defiance.

"It's not a request, Barlow." Jack was serious and Barlow knew it. Barlow wasn't tough without his little army and had no choice except to do it. He handed the boots and pants to the saloon girl who reluctantly said she'd take care of them for him. His red long johns were wet too, but Jack thought that would be going too far.

Barlow went to mount his horse but Jack stopped him. "Sorry, Brad, the horse stays."

Barlow's face dropped. "Mr. McCall, it's over twelve miles back to my ranch."

"Is that a fact? Well, then my suggestion to you is, use that time to consider the error of your ways." Jack's face turned serious. "On your way, Barlow!"

Barlow walked out of town to the delight and the amusement of the townfolk. They could hear him cursing all the way through town.

Dan looked to Jack. "You really think that Brad Barlow will consider anything other than a way to get even with you?"

"Of course not. I just wanted enough time to get Chota's medicine and get out of here."

"Good idea, Jack. Let's get moving."

Chapter Four
Mission San Xavier

It didn't take long for Jack and his two companions to leave town. Jack knew it wasn't a question if Barlow would seek vengence, but only a question of how soon and in what form. He also knew that his odds were much better out in the desert. He didn't like being in the close quarters of the town, where a back-shooter has plenty of cover and opportunity. So, they finished up their business in Tucson quickly.

Jack had no trouble convincing the drugist to let Chota have anything he wanted. While Chota was getting the medicine, Jack stood outside with a watchful eye. When his Indian friend had finished, Jack went back in and settled the account. He then explained to Chota that later, when they weren't in such a hurry, he would sell McBride's things to recoup his money. This was acceptable to Chota's sense of honesty.

They then stopped at the livery. The stable had a few wagons and buggies for hire. They also had a decent-looking saddle horse for rent. If they were to make any sort of speed and stay ahead of Barlow's men, Chota would need a horse. Because the owner knew Dan pretty well, he made Jack a good deal on the buckskin mare, four dollars for up to a week. *Plenty of time,* Jack thought. *Time to get Chota safely back to his village and then figure a way to deal with Barlow.* Once again, he told Chota that it was just a loan and that seemed to satisfy the proud Indian. Jack busied himself saddling Chota's mount and his own, the big palomino, Chilco. Dan's horse was also stabled there at the livery. He quickly had it saddled. It was a smallish paint that he called Patches. Jack and Dan settled up with the livery owner and then they all rode back to the Longhorn.

They gathered and packed their gear. Chota had his saddlebags filled with the just purchased medicine. Since Jack always carried his city duds, he had them folded up in his left bag. The right one carried his supply of cartridges. Dan was accustomed to traveling light, so he ended up packing McBride's things. After a quick adios to the barkeeper, they saddled up and headed south.

As they rode, they could see the hills and mountains in the distance. Behind them, the structures that made up Tucson became ever smaller and then, after a while, disappeared. It was a fairly warm morning with bright, clear skies. The wide-open desert scene of cactus, mesquite, and sage gave Jack a sense of relief. If trouble came, he'd have time to react. Riding along in that open country also reminded him of why he'd left the show. He simply missed the trail and the feeling of freedom.

Chota had told Jack and Dan very little about his village or even where it was. He did say that they would pass through Mission San Xavier. That would be their first stop, about two hours out of Tucson. There they would get supplies from the local Indians. The Papago tribe were peaceful farmers. The name Papago meant "bean" people, for that was their primary crop. They sold food supplies and other Indian wares to ranchers, miners, and passersby.

Dan was riding between Chota and Jack. They had left Tucson without having breakfast and Dan's stomach was starting to grumble. He looked left over at Chota. "You dealt with these Papagos before, Chota?"

Chota nodded, "Yes, I know them."

"What sort of grub they got there? I'm getting hungry!" he rubbed his belly.

"We'll get beans, tortillas, and vegetables there," he answered with a slight smile.

"Boy, Chota, I could use some of those frijoles and tortillas right now. How about you, Jack?" he turned toward him. Jack gave him a little grin and nodded. Then he looked across at Chota. "How much farther is it to your village from the Mission?"

Chota didn't answer for a few minutes. At first, Jack thought he hadn't heard him because his attention seemed elsewhere. Then he answered, but his words seemed to come with some reluctance.

"You not have to go whole way. When safe, I give you back this horse. You not need to go whole way." His eyes seemed fixed on something in the distance.

Jack studied Chota's face and tried to figure what his concerns might be. Was it that he felt obliged and thought he was imposing on his friends? Was it simply pride? Somehow, Jack felt it was something else, but he was a difficult man to read. If it was only that Chota didn't want Dan and him to feel put-upon, then Jack wanted to assure him otherwise. "Well, Chota, you know we'll let you go on by yourself if that's what you really want. But as for me, and I'm sure for Dan too, we'd just as soon ride along with you. Right, Dan?"

"You betcha. We'd be proud to ride all the way with you partner!" Dan returned with enthusiasm.

Chota lowered his head a little and then seemed to focus on something in the distance. His silence and distraction puzzled his friends.

Jack liked Chota. He impressed Jack as a good and honorable man. He felt genuine warmth from Chota and a growing trust. But where he felt an immediate openness between himself and Dan, this was not true of his Indian friend. There was definitely a limit on just how close he could get to Chota, and just how much he wanted known about himself. Jack wondered if it was just the Indian's way, or if there was more to it than that. The three men spoke little the rest of the way to the mission.

Mission San Xavier was built in the late eighteenth century. It was constructed with stone and adobe and covered with smooth cement. Jack was impressed by the beauty of the place. There were two high towers, with an ornate façade between them. The mission was not difficult to find. It could be seen many miles away in any direction. The missionaries had left years earlier, but the Papagos made good use of it.

As Jack and company approached, they could see that it was the center point of the Papago tribe. There were huts scattered all around the mission. These small huts that they lived in had flat top roofs. Some were made of woven ocotillo and others were of Saguaro wood.

There was a profusion of activity. Women were cooking, grinding corn, and making baskets. Children were playing and dogs were here and there. The younger men were still out in the fields.

Many of the older people were tending to infants. Near the entrance to the mission, there was an area where the tribe did business. Laid out on mats and blankets, and in large baskets were vegetables, corn, wheat flour, and a type of tortilla. They also had blankets and baskets for sale. There were a few mesquite fires going behind the vendors and there were women willing to fry up an Indian meal upon request. Dan wasted little time in doing just that. While Dan ordered vittles for three, Jack watched the comings and goings of tribal life with interest.

The Papago Indians were a happy and industrious people. Jack noticed that there were few farm animals, some goats and sheep but no horses. He also noticed that Chota seemed to know these people pretty well, and he had no trouble speaking to them in their language.

Dan called and motioned his two pals to join him on a long blanket. A rather large and cheerful woman gave them shallow bowls with beans, corn, and tortillas. It was time to eat, and they were all hungry. Jack was glad to see that Chota could put away food. He seemed to be a bit stronger than the previous night but still pale for an Indian.

About halfway through what was a surprisingly good meal, they heard a commotion and looked in that direction. There was a group of excited people forming around what appeared to be a frantic young boy a small distance away, by some huts. Jack sensed that whatever the trouble was, it was serious. He felt a little helpless, though, not knowing the language. Just as he started to ask his Indian friend to look into it, he noticed that Chota was already on his feet. Immediately, he headed over to the growing crowd with what speed he could manage.

Jack and Dan watched as Chota spoke to several people and saw each one point to the young boy and down toward the river. Chota hurried back with a very solemn expression on his face. Dan and Jack stood up, figuring it wasn't going to be good news. Chota stopped a little before them and took a deep breath. Not yet back to his full strength, he had gotten a little winded. "Miners take girl away, down by river," he announced in an excited and labored voice.

"How long ago and how many men?" queried Jack. Dan and Chota could see anger growing in Jack's eyes.

"Not long. See that boy over there?" Chota pointed toward the boy within the excited crowd. "He went down to river to get water. He got there in time to see two miners ride away with girl."

"Just two men?" asked Jack, while he wondered why people were staring at them.

"Just two," replied Chota.

"Tell those people I'll bring the girl back and take care of those men."

"I tell them that already." Chota wore a wry

smile. Jack's eyebrows raised. "Ah! That explains all those looks we're getting. Either of you have any idea where those miners will be heading?"

Dan's eyes moved to Chota. "Were those miners here for supplies?"

"Yes, people saw them here this morning."

"Then I know where they're going, Jack." Dan pointed toward the river. "Look down at the river where that boy saw the miners nab the girl." They both looked. "Now, look beyond that, at the dark mountain in the distance. At the foot of that mountain, in a canyon, there are about a dozen silver mines, maybe a half day's ride from here."

Chota nodded in agreement. "Yes, Dan's right. Miners come here for supplies."

"Good." Jack put his hand on Chota's shoulder. "Do you want to ride along or stay here and deal with the Papagos for supplies?"

Chota shook his head. "I might slow you down. You get girl quick. I wait here, be ready to leave when you return."

Jack simply nodded and headed for his horse. Dan gave Chota a little slap on the back and stated, "We'll be back before you know it partner." Then he turned toward his horse and grinned. "Boy, do those miners have a surprise coming."

Chapter Five
Apache Justice

Jack and Dan rode down to the tree-lined river at a full gallop. They crossed the very shallow Santa Cruz River and headed southeast, in the direction of the silver mines. Since they knew where the miners were heading, they didn't have to waste time finding and following their trail. Jack also figured that the miners would know that the Papagos didn't have horses in which to give chase. In fact, Jack thought it likely that the miners didn't know that someone had seen them take the girl. So it was quite possible they wouldn't be riding too hard. All the same, they pushed at a rapid rate, with Dan leading the way. Jack was happy to let Dan take charge because he certainly knew more about this terrain than he did. Southern Arizona was one of the places he'd not gotten around to before. That's why he'd chosen Tucson as the place to leave the show. He wanted to start in country that was new to him.

After a while, they could see a little dust ahead and off to their right. Dan slowed his pony down to a trot and Jack sided him. "That's got to be them, Jack." He motioned toward the dust. "They're riding down in a wash. We can't see them and they can't see us."

"Can we get ahead of them without them knowing it?" Jack was noticing that he and Dan's horses were also making dust.

"Yep, I think we can. If we mosey over to our left, we can get on to that red clay over there." Dan gestured toward a copper-colored band of earth going up a rise off in the distance. "That clay don't make dust worth squat."

"So we'll get enough ahead so we can cut them off slow and easy and keep the dust down."

"That's the idea."

"Lead the way, Dan."

They kept the horses to a slow trot until they reached the red clay. Then they turned right and gave their horses their heads. Jack looked back with a satisfied grin. Barely a trace of dust.

If it wasn't for the urgency of catching the miners, Jack would have appreciated the scenery. The streak of copper-colored clay they were riding on was fairly wide. It appeared to go all the way to a tall and rugged mountain, miles away in the distance. There were varied patches and bands of lighter and darker colored ground running mostly in the same direction as the red clay. Although the general terrain was going gently up to meet the mountain ahead in the distance, it wasn't flat. There were a series of rises and gullies and the wash that concealed the miners, but not their dust, which was now a ways behind.

There was brush, but it was sparse. The cactus was more abundant. It came as small as a stubby barrel cactus and as large as the stately Saguaro. The stark beauty and contrast of the desert was mostly unnoticed by Jack, but something else was not. Looking ahead, he could see a gully that angled off to the right. It seemed to head right for the wash that the miners were riding in. As Jack got closer, he could see it did join up with the wash and it cut right through its left wall. The gully was a tributary to the wash, although that day, it would serve as Jack and Dan's entrance.

Dan saw Jack's interest in the gully. He looked back and could see that the dust trail was safely behind them. He slowed his horse down to a fast walk. Jack rode up on his right side. "I know what you're thinking, Jack." He looked over where the gully cut into the wash a little ways ahead.

"That's part of it, Dan, but I've been giving those two miners some thought."

"What's to think about? They're just miners, Jack! You could beat them galutes with your eyes closed." He wore a puzzled look.

Jack slowed Chilco to a walk, to keep down the dust and turned to go into the gully. Dan came back up on his left. Jack glanced over at his friend. "Getting the girl back isn't the problem, Dan. The problem is what to do with those men. Sure, I could kill them, but I don't want to. We don't have time to bring them in to the law, and that would take us back to town."

"Not only that, Jack, but you can't count on the law around here caring two hoots about an Indian. They'd probably end up giving them miners a medal." It was an exaggeration, but Jack knew Dan wasn't far off.

They were riding slowly side-by-side in the gully now. In a few minutes they would reach the wash. Jack looked over at Dan again. "So, we need to teach these two hombres a lesson, ourselves. We need to scare the bajesus out of those no-goods! I want to give them something they won't soon forget."

Dan smiled and as they rode the final way to the wash, Jack explained his plan. As Dan heard the scheme, his smile turned into a big grin.

Jack and Dan waited in the gully just out of sight of the approaching miners. When they sounded like they were getting fairly close, Jack and Dan nonchalantly walked their horses into the wash, turned and faced the on-coming riders. The wash, which had been carved over the ages into a small canyon, had broken red clay walls, a brown sandy bottom with assorted rocks and brush. There were two bearded men, both on chestnut mounts, with two horses led behind. One horse, a gray, was packing supplies. On the other horse, a bay, was the Indian girl. She looked very uncomfortable. She was perched upon an already loaded pack-horse and her hands were tied. She also looked quite beautiful. She was small and probably not more than twenty years old, Jack thought. He also thought that she was the most striking female he'd ever seen. He quickly decided not to think anymore about that or really look her way until he finished dealing with those two no-accounts.

The miners had been riding at a trot. They slowed and stopped just in front of Jack and Dan. The man on the left could best be described as rangy. He was tall and had a dark beard. He wore his plaid shirt open at the top and had a pistol tucked into his gray pants. The man to Jack's right was husky. His face was round and his beard was brown. Black suspenders went over a stained dark blue shirt and attached to denim trousers. Jack couldn't see a sidearm on this man, but the man had his hand on a saddle-mounted Winchester. Both men wore sweat-stained gray Stetsons. Neither looked like they were a threat with a gun.

In that moment, when they first stopped and faced each other, Jack could see that the miners were nervous. The rangy one spoke first in a high wispy tone. "You men just passing by, or you want something?" he asked with suspicion.

"I want something," answered Jack flatly.

The husky man had fear in his eyes, he spoke softly. "We ain't got money, mister." His voice was deep and wavered some. "What do you want from us?" He could see from Jack's look and the hardware he carried that they were outmatched. "We ain't looking for trouble."

"Well, you've got trouble, mister!" Jack's face gave away nothing. "You just don't know how much." His stare was locked onto the two scared miners. He motioned toward the girl. "Take care of the girl, Dan."

"Sure thing, Jack," and Dan stepped off his horse.

The rangy man must have thought that with one adversary in the midst of dismounting it was his best chance, for in that moment, it was two against one. He reached for the pistol tucked into the waist of his pants. He maybe touched one or two fingers on the handle, when there was what sounded like one very loud gunshot. It was really two shots fired at exactly the same time, one from each of Jack's .45s. The result of these two bullets, besides scaring the wits out of both miners, was two ventilated sweat-stained Stetsons flying in the air and settling onto the ground.

Jack kept the two smoking Colts aimed at their heads. The two miners with blinking, glazed eyes, seemed to be quivering in unison. Both were terrified and dazed by such speed. Dan chuckled as he walked over to set the girl free. Jack settled back into his saddle and then used the barrel of his left gun to tip his black Stetson a little back on his head. "Alright, boys, chuck the iron on the ground." A pistol and rifle hit the earth. Jack spun his Colts back into their holsters. "I want to talk to you boys a little first," he stated calmly.

The rangy cus stammered out, "Before what, Mister?" His voice was even higher than before.

"We'll get to that." Jack answered impatiently. "Now, why'd you take the girl?"

They looked at each other nervously, and somehow without speaking, decided that Rangy would speak for them. "We know it was wrong, mister, but it gets really cold out here at night sleeping in a tent." They tried to offer a little smile. "We weren't gonna hurt her none, honest, mister." At the same time, Dan was helping the girl over to the left side of the wash and sat her down. Before Rangy continued, he glanced at the girl and then quickly back to Jack. "Besides, why all the fuss? She's just an Injun." He really seemed perplexed.

Before Jack could speak, Dan walked up to the

rangy cus and looked coldly up at him. "You better watch what you two are saying." He motioned toward Jack. "You know who he is?" They both shook their heads. "Diamondback McCall," he answered with satisfaction. "Not only is he the fastest gun and surest shot ever to draw a breath, he's also an Indian." Dan nodded and gave his best fierce look. The husky galute looked at his partner and said quietly, "He don't look like no Injun." While the two miners gave Jack another look, Jack made a broad gesture to Dan.

"Go find them now, Dan."

"I'll find some, Jack, don't worry." Behind where the girl was sitting, the red clay wall had tumbled down at sometime in the past and it left a rugged path to the top. Dan turned, walked past the girl and started making his way up and out of the wash.

Jack returned his harsh stare at the miners. "You don't think I'm Indian?" His voice was cold.

The husky man thought he had said it softly enough that Jack didn't hear him and he was terrified. "I'm sorry, Mr. McCall, sir, but to be honest," he paused and swallowed, "you don't look Indian."

"My mother was Indian! Full-blooded Apache!" Jack returned defiantly. He looked over at the frightened and still trembling girl. He then returned his stare at the miners. He and Dan were doing some acting for the benefit of the two kidnappers, but the anger he felt toward them for what they had done and what they planned to do to her was real enough.

The rangy man could see Jack's anger. "You're not gonna shoot us, are you?"

"Your crime was committed against an Indian and we'll settle it in the Indian way. In fact, the Apache way. So no, I'm not going to shoot you." Jack gave a thin smile.

"So, what are you gonna do to us, mister?" Rangy was almost in tears.

"You'll see," was Jack's terse response. The miners gave each other an empty stare.

"Now step down off of those ponies, boys." The miners kept looking at each other and hesitated. "Now!" Jack demanded and they dismounted quickly.

"Now, go over by the girl," he stated firmly, and as they complied, Jack stepped down from his horse. He took his rope from the saddle and walked over to the miners. By then, they were standing by the girl and facing him. "Turn around and put your hands behind you."

They didn't like it, but they obeyed. Jack tied their hands securely and then looked up at Dan, who was walking around above the wash. He was looking down like he was trying to find something.

"Any luck, Dan?" Jack called up to him.

"Not yet!" Dan fired back.

The two miners were now as concerned about

what Dan was up to as they were about being tied up. The larger man stared at Dan. "Ah, Mr. McCall, sir," the waver in his voice went up at the end, "what's he doing up there?"

Jack couldn't resist a smile. "Well, Dan's up there arranging for lunch, boys," his smile grew, "and you two are the guests of honor."

"So, what's he looking for, mister? I mean, what do you expect us to eat?" The husky man asked nervously, as they both turned back toward Jack.

Jack shook his head, "You boys got it all wrong. You're not having lunch," he paused for effect. "You are lunch!" The miners gasped and seemed to deteriorate even further.

Jack looked back up at Dan. "Any luck yet, partner?"

"Yep, found some. Will red ones do, Jack?"

"They'll do fine, Dan. Now, come on back down and get the molasses out of your saddlebag and we'll get these gentlemen ready for the ants."

After a moment of disbelief, terror flushed across the two men's faces and they both cried out, "NO!" They fell to their knees and began blubbering for mercy at Jack's feet.

As Jack looked down and listened to the pathetic pleas from the miners, he noticed that the girl had suddenly stood up and was looking at him. His eyes were captivated by her lovely face. Her eyes were filled with concern. Her voice was soft and high, and her words were pronounced with articulate English. "They're not worth it," she looked down at the sobbing miners, looked back at Jack and stepped near him. "Don't do this, please!" Her pretty face was tense. Her dark sensitive eyes began to tear. "Not for me, I'm alright. Not for you, you'll have to live with this."

Jack gave her a nod. He felt that the stake the miners to an anthill routine had gone far enough. He also didn't want to cause this lovely girl any more distress.

He looked down at the two miners. "I guess this is your lucky day. For some reason, the lady doesn't want you two eaten alive. It's sure not my idea. I personally think you've got it coming."

The sobbing diminished and the two men looked gratefully at the girl. She, understandably, turned away from them. Her compassion was real, but her contempt for them was equally real.

Jack motioned for Dan to come back down. While he descended along the tumbled down wall, Jack untied the two miners. "On your feet, boys!"

They stood up slowly, and as Jack nudged them to turn around, he could see the look of relief on their faces. "Alright, boys. You two are walking away from this with your hides, but not much else. You're giving this girl and her people your horses and supplies. This will be restitution for what you did. And it's not nearly enough! You two agree with this?"

They both nodded and Rangy managed to mutter, "That's fair Mr. McCall."

"Good, then there are just two more details," stated Jack. By this time, Dan had made it back and was standing near the girl. Jack looked over his shoulder at him. "Dan, why don't you see if you can find about a week's worth of beans and flour from one of those packhorses."

Dan nodded and went over to see what he could find.

Jack then focused on the two miners. He stared coldly into their eyes. "Alright, you two! First thing, and you better not forget it. If you ever pull anything like this again, especially against Indians or a woman, I'll hear about it." Jack expression was stern and the two men seemed to be buying his sincerity. But to make his point absolutely clear, he drew his two Colts, put the barrels against each man's nose and cocked both hammers just to emphasize his last point. "And then, I'll hunt you down and feed you to the ants! Comprende?"

"Oh yes, yes and yes, sir," stumbled out of both men's mouths at once.

Jack spun his Colts back into his holsters and gave a terse nod.

Dan then walked up to the miners carrying the

two sacks Jack had asked for. He held them out to the miners. The husky one accepted them. "Like Jack said," Dan began, "there's one more thing. Give me your britches." He looked at the confused faces of the two men for a moment, and then raised his voice. "Take off your pants and hand them to me!"

They didn't speak. They just looked at Dan and then looked over to Jack.

In response, Jack simply drew the two Colts out again and stated, "Do it!"

Dan and Jack had carried out their acting performance for the miners pretty well, so far. Now as the miners removed their trousers, it was getting difficult for Dan to keep a straight face. They were both wearing old, faded red long johns. But the trap door on the back of the rangy man's pair had no buttons and was hanging wide open. Dan had to turn away for a bit to compose himself. He forced a serious expression and then turned back around just in time to receive the two trousers. He held one pair in each hand and noticed a considerable difference in weight. In the right front pocket of the pants in his left hand was a small pouch of silver. Dan took the pouch from the pocket and tossed it to the husky man who was closer. "I don't want your money, just your britches." He couldn't contain a little chuckle, "Now get!"

The two men turned and started walking. It was

a peculiar sight, both in long johns, and one exposing his rear.

"You can pick up your hats and weapons," announced Jack.

They gathered their Stetsons and hardware and then both men looked back at Jack.

"You'll need those guns for rabbits and such," Jack continued, "or did you have something else in mind?"

They shook their heads and turned for home.

"You can move faster than that!" Dan called out. He pulled McBride's pistol out and fired one shot over their heads. They took off at a dead run.

Dan smiled at his partner, "Dang that felt good." He slid the six-gun back into its holster and the smile grew. "And mighty interesting, Jack."

Chapter Six
Lousy Odds

The day was slipping away. The time it had taken to catch and deal with the miners was considerable. This detour could have lost them their time advantage over Barlow and his hired guns. Jack knew he would have to keep scanning into the distance for any sign of riders. Dan went about tying a lead from one pack horse to Jack's horse, and then tied the other pack horse plus Husky's horse to his mount. While Dan was doing this, Jack helped the girl up onto Rangy's horse and adjusted the stirrups. Jack didn't make the mistake the miners did. He led them out of the wash to high ground, so he could see if anyone was coming. They headed back toward the mission.

They rode side-by-side, Jack on the left of the

girl, Dan to her right. Jack noticed that she seemed to be calm and pretty much recovered from her ordeal. He also noticed a big grin growing on Dan's face. Dan looked left over at his partner and laughed out loud. "We really did it, Jack!" He laughed again. "Why, we played those two like a gypsy plays a fiddle! Scared the pants off of them too, and I've got the pants to prove it." He chuckled and tapped his left saddlebag which contained his growing collection of trousers.

Jack nodded back at his friend, "Yeah, I think they learned a lesson, I just hope they remember it."

"I think you can count on that. I got a good look at their eyes. You've got the Indian sign on those two." Dan realized what he had said and felt a little ashamed about it. Of course, Jack did have a kind of power or control over the miners, much like a spell. Dan still wished he'd said it differently. "No offense Miss," he gave the girl an awkward smile, "or is it missus?"

"No offense taken, and it's Miss. But just call me Fawn." She then added, "And thank you for, well, for everything." She smiled at both men but then they could see her expression turn quizzical. "Were you men just acting back there? You made it sound like you were planning on letting them go all the time." She posed the question to both of them but she was looking at Jack.

He couldn't hold back a little grin. "Just an act,

just a bluff." He motioned toward his partner. "Dan and I, that's Dakota Dan Smith, by the way."

Dan tipped his Stetson.

"Well, we cooked all that up so they'd think twice about trying something like that again."

Dan shook his head, "Heck, it weren't none of my idea. Jack thought up the whole dang thing. But it sure had those two goin'," he nodded at the girl.

"It had me going too." Her eyes moved from Dan to Jack. "I guess you could tell, I really thought you were going to feed those miners to the ants."

"Oh, we wouldn't do that," he gave her a little wink, "with those two, it would have probably made the ants sick."

She laughed and gave him an affectionate glance.

Jack was taken with this girl. She was sweet, sincere, and bright. Her face was charming and lovely. Her long black hair was worn loose and fell to her waist. An attractive silver and turquoise necklace adorned her equally pretty neck. The plain white cotton dress she wore revealed a delicately pleasing shape that moved with the horse. It also seemed to move Jack.

Jack's eyes made a one hundred eighty degree sweep of the desert and then he turned to the girl. "So, Fawn," he thought the name was appropriate, "where did you learn your English? It's very good."

Her face turned serious and she dropped her head a little. "Well, when I was little, there was an outbreak of influenza and I lost my parents. At the time, the Smiths, who owned the Santa Rosita Ranch, lost their little girl in the same way. Well, John and Helen Smith would come by the mission for supplies and they heard about me. So they took me in and I lived with them on the ranch until they lost it about six months ago."

She glanced at Jack and Dan and could see they were interested, so she continued. "Helen taught school in St. Louis before they came out here and she liked teaching me. In fact, she made me want to teach too. So when they were forced to sell, they went back to Missouri and I decided to come back to my people and try teaching the children at the mission."

Dan was shaking his head, "I heard about the Smiths losing their spread, and they were nice folks, by all accounts. And they weren't the only ones forced to sell for cheap." Dan looked over at his partner. "Of course, it was that no-good rattlesnake Barlow and his men."

"I guess we should have mentioned that Barlow is probably after us, right now." Jack spoke to her apologetically. "We had a run-in with him this morning. Being with us might not be the safest place in the whole world right now."

She seemed to quiver in the saddle. "That Barlow!" she said with disdain. "He'd come to the ranch with his men to put a scare into the Smiths.

And he'd always stare at me." She shook her head. "He's like a spider!" She looked over to Jack and pursed her lips. "If Barlow's around, I don't want to be out here alone." Then her mouth managed a crooked little smile. "Besides, I trust you." She nodded, "I'll stay with you."

Jack returned the nod, and they rode on. They kept the horses to a fast walk, not wanting to tire them unnecessarily. It was a pleasant enough day, Jack thought, warm but not hot. There were some wispy clouds moving slowly overhead. The sun felt good against a westerly breeze. Time was going by slowly as they traveled across the open desert. Jack and Fawn exchanged fond looks from time to time. For the most part, of course, he looked out in the direction of Tucson and the mission. He had hoped that there would be nothing to see, but there was.

In the direction of the mission, he could see a thin trail of dust. *That's no whirlwind,* he said to himself. He focused on the dust and concluded it was a rider, just one rider, coming their way.

Pretty soon Dan picked up on Jack's concern, and he too watched the dust several miles ahead. "Somebody's in one heck of a hurry, partner."

"You're right about that, Dan. Whoever's coming is using up his horse fast!"

"Yep, but it don't make a heap of sense, unless . . ."

"Unless he's being chased?"

"Uh oh," Dan said under his breath.

Jack peered hard and, after some time, finally recognized the rider. "Chota!" he announced. Then he motioned toward the horses Dan was leading. "He's going to need a fresh mount, Dan."

He nodded and got to it. He untied the saddled horse and tied the packhorse onto his. He remounted holding Chota's new mount by the bridle. "All set, Jack," Dan stated, and all three watched Chota's fast approach. He then slowed and stopped just in front of them. As the dust settled over them, it was plain to see that Chota was quite agitated and more than a little winded.

He took a deep breath. "Men come to mission looking for us!" he gulped some more air. "I lucky to get away." He then turned and pointed behind him. "But now they come," he turned back and looked remorsefully at Jack. "I wanted to warn you. I only lead them to you." His voice had a ring of despair.

"It's not your fault, Chota," Jack acknowledged. "I shouldn't have left you behind." He motioned for Dan to bring the fresh horse to Chota but his attention was on what was a very large dust cloud. While Chota switched mounts, Jack tried to judge the distance. "Could you see how many men, Chota?" His eyes remained on the growing cloud.

"I think thirty. Maybe more," he answered but his eyes seemed fixed on some point in the mountains behind them.

Jack spun his horse around to face Dan. "I figure we've got maybe twenty minutes before they're on top of us, what do you think?" His words came softly and calmly so he wouldn't convey panic to the others.

"No more than that, Jack."

"We've got no chance against that many out here in the open. We'll have to make a run for some place defendable. Any ideas?"

Dan pointed to the Santa Rita behind them. "We can reach those mountains in probably two hours or so if we push it. But I'm none too sure you're gonna find what you're lookin' for there." His words were steady but Jack saw something in his eyes he'd not seen before. Fear was certainly understandable. The odds were lousy, and Dan knew this all too well.

Going against the odds, however, was nothing new to Jack McCall. Although one man going up against thirty or more guns in the open desert seemed a foolish venture, if he were alone, Jack might have tried it. With his ability with a Winchester, he could stage hit and run tactics, staying just beyond their range. The idea being to frustrate and discourage the larger force. It's a desperate measure and risky because of the volume of fire from his adversaries. But he wasn't alone. So, he couldn't take the chance that one of Barlow's men might get in a lucky shot. That would leave Fawn and the others at the mercy of Barlow.

There had to be some way to protect Fawn and his friends. Jack found himself momentarily gazing into Fawn's frightened eyes. Then he looked toward the Santa Rita range. "Alright, then. We'll ride due east to those mountains and figure it out when we get there." He knew that didn't sound optimistic, but that was the situation. He started to turn his horse east, when Chota suddenly shook his head and yelled, "No! I know safe place," he said firmly and pointed southeast. "See, there are two sharp peaks where two mountains come together." They could easily see the two majestic spires, one on each mountain crest. Where the two mountains met, the hillsides sloped down to form what looked like maybe a little canyon. Still, from this distance, they could not see the detail.

"We ride there and Chota show safe place!"

There were no questions or even words from the others. If Chota knew of a safe place, then that was good enough.

Jack motioned for Chota to lead the way with a wide sweep of his left hand. They all took off at a gallop, except for Chota's earlier mount, which like all horses, would find its way back to the barn, or in this case, the livery.

They rode hard but at a sustainable pace. They

had a couple of advantages over their pursuers. They had some distance on them and fresher horses. Barlow's little army had been charging for quite a while. As Chota took them across the flat to undulating terrain, Jack noticed a few things. He could see that Chota was not exactly at home on a galloping horse, holding tight on the saddle horn and not getting in rhythm with the animal's motion. Chota would likely be sore tonight, Jack noted. However, Chota certainly knew the lay of the land. He followed a smooth and fast route that indicated that he knew the area very well.

Jack also noticed the approaching mountains and the sun. He calculated the location of both. He hoped Chota was right about that safe place, for he figured that by the time they reached the mountains, there'd still be at least another hour of light. They wouldn't have the cover of darkness.

The ground that they traveled upon was an ever-changing surface. It varied from hard to sandy to rocky and even some fairly soft clay. Barlow's riders were not gaining any distance, but they weren't losing any either. Chota and company had held off their chasers for a little over an hour when they rode into one of the more rocky areas. The ground was firm but strewn with small rocks and stones. Chota had been leading the way, but he wasn't experienced with horses. If Jack or Dan were at the front, they would have immediately slowed everyone way down to protect the horses' hooves. As it happened, when they came upon the rocky ground, both Dan and Jack shouted for the others to slow down, but it wasn't soon enough.

Fawn's horse stumbled badly and nearly pitched her off. In that moment when the horse stumbled, the speed was such that the horse actually came down on its left front knee. This violent action caused Fawn to be thrown forward and left in the same instant. The horse righted itself and limped to a stop. Fawn found herself halfway up the horses neck. Her right leg was bent around the saddle horn, her left foot was against the horse's chest, while her grip of the mane was all that kept her from falling. Jack rode up beside her and leapt to the ground. In two steps, he was there with his arms beneath her.

"I've got you," he seemed slightly amused by her position and predicament. She gave him an embarrassed frown and then fell into his arms. There was a moment when they found themselves lost in each other's eyes.

In those few seconds, Jack felt something he had not felt before. Just as quickly, however, reality swept over him. "Are you all right?" he smiled fondly.

She smiled back. "I'm fine, but what about the horse?"

"Let me take a look," Jack said soberly as he gently put Fawn down to her feet. He knelt by the animal and felt its suspect leg. He quickly examined the knee, ankle and inner hoof. "Not real serious," he announced to the others. "But it can't be ridden."

He then briskly went to Chilco and swung up into the saddle. He turned the horse for Fawn to join him, bent down, and offered an outstretched hand. "You'll have to ride behind me."

She extended both hands and clasped his. In one smooth powerful motion, he lifted her and set her down easy on the horse's hind quarters.

"That cost us some time Chota, but you'll have to keep the speed down until we clear these rocks."

Chota nodded and Jack took a survey of their pursuers. It wasn't just dust he saw anymore. He could actually see riders. It was getting a little close.

The rocky little plain they had found themselves on was crossed in only a few minutes. From that point and as far as could be seen in the direction of the mountains was typical hard to sandy ground. The lame horse was left behind, as Chota once again led the way. He took a fairly straight course toward the two spires atop the mountains he had indicated earlier. They all had to do a certain amount of negotiation of the terrain as they went along. They dodged holes and cactus. Small ruts could be jumped, while large gullies required a careful approach. The mountains loomed larger, and as they reached the foothills, the ascent got steeper. Brush took over from the cactus that was dominant in the lower desert plain. The pace slowed as the climbing got tougher.

They seemed to be heading for the canyon between the two spires. From what Jack could see, the canyon looked quite narrow with very high walls. As they got closer, it looked like they'd probably have to funnel down to single file inside the canyon. He wondered if that was Chota's plan, to get there first and only have to face one or two men at a time. Jack looked back at the very persistent enemy.

Such tenacity had surprised him. For them to push this hard and this long, Jack concluded, there must be a very large price on his head. He also found it appalling that they had such little regard for their horses. On the other hand, their persistence seemed to be paying off. Barlow's men were just now reaching the steeper point of the foothills. So, for a while, they had been going faster than their prey, who were, because of the steep climb, going pretty slow. The gap was getting uncomfortably smaller.

Barlow's men also must have realized that the narrow canyon was the destination, and decided not to wait until they reached it. Shots rang out from Barlow's men. It was still a bit beyond the range of their rifles, and they were using Kentucky windage to try and get in a lucky hit. Most of the spent bullets were falling short but others were getting too close. Jack knew, even at that distance, the sheer volume of fire meant someone would be hit if this continued. He glanced over his shoulder at Fawn. "Can you get me the box of cartridges in my right saddlebag?"

She retrieved them, and handed them to him around his waist. "What are you going to do?" There was worry in the tone of her voice.

He pulled out his Winchester, threw his right leg over Chilco's neck and jumped off. As he struck the ground, he shouted, "Get into that canyon, fast! I'll detain our friends." Jack watched as Fawn slipped forward into Chilco's saddle. He noted that they did manage a little more speed out of the horses. As they climbed the brush-covered rise toward the canyon between two spired mountains, Jack knelt behind one of the larger sagebrush specimens, opened the cartridge box and cocked the rifle. Bullets continued to fly toward Jack from Barlow's men. Now it was their turn.

Accuracy with a rifle aboard a horse in motion is difficult. When the horse is going up hill, it's doubly so. The pitching action of a horse's back when climbing is extreme. Barlow's men were banking on their weight of fire landing random hits. They knew if they were to stop to take careful aim that the distance would open up and they'd be completely out of range. Jack knew this too.

Jack also knew the art of Kentucky windage as well as anyone. He figured for this distance, he'd aim four feet over their heads. It was long range even for him. Jack could empty a Winchester in five seconds and reload in eight. He opened up on them. By the time he was reloading the second time, not a single one of Barlow's men were on a horse. They had all dived off and spread out for cover. Jack's main intention was complete, his friends were now out of range.

It must have been obvious to Barlow's men who was firing at them. They now had Jack on foot. There was plenty of brush cover, and they knew that this was their best chance.

Jack's plan was simple; fire a pattern across their position and then hightail it back to another large sagebrush before they could recover. He hoped to keep this hit and run tactic up until he too was out of range. But someone in Barlow's private little army had to have spent some time in the real army, Jack thought. They split their force. Then, while the left side laid down cover fire, the right side moved out and forward. Then the roles were reversed and the left side came up and around. It was a classic flanking maneuver and it was keeping Jack pinned flat on his stomach by organized continual fire. Jack could see that the enemy would soon be close and have him in a cross fire.

The breeze was still blowing west. In fact, the wind had picked up, and west was the direction of Barlow's men. If you're traveling any distance by horse, you carry matches for campfires. Jack started rolling from bush to bush, lighting them afire. The brush was kindling timber dry, and so close together that it didn't take very long to have a swath of flame and smoke heading for the gunmen. Sage brush makes a particularly dark and sooty smoke, but it also burns very fast. Jack had to move back quickly because as the wind carried the fire away from him, so went the smoke that now concealed him. He also had to be careful, for the smoke not only covered his movement, it also, just as effectively, covered theirs.

Barlow's men stopped firing. That could mean they were momentarily confused, or it could be that they were on the move. Either way, Jack knew it was time to go. He ran in a crouch and moved side-to-side. After a half minute or so, he ducked behind another large sagebrush and surveyed the enemy line. The fire was raging with plumes of smoke and moving steadily toward Barlow's men's position. But here and there, Jack could see the men, through spots where the smoke was thinner, making their way around the fire. They definitely hadn't given up.

Then suddenly, his attention was diverted by a most unexpected sound from an unexpected direction. The thudding sound of galloping hooves bearing down on him from behind. He spun around with his Winchester aimed at the oncoming rider. Then, as he focused on what was coming his way, he had a feeling of both shock and relief at the same time. It was Fawn on board Chilco, charging right for him. She pulled the big horse to a stop in front of him and turned Chilco around. Jack ran only three steps and bounded up on Chilco's hind quarters, just like he'd done so many times before in the show. But unlike the show, bullets started whizzing at them again.

Some of Barlow's men had made it around the smoke and had a clear view of them above the brush. It was only a few men firing at them, though, and Chilco quickly had Fawn and Jack out of range.

They were safe for now, and heading for the canyon. This was the bravest girl Jack had ever known. He felt her trembling, yet she had done it anyway. He put his hand on her shoulder. No words were necessary.

Chapter Seven
Hideout

When they reached the entrance to the canyon, it wasn't what Jack thought it would be. From a distance, it had looked like a narrow canyon that went between the mountains. But it was actually a box canyon. It was all rock. Rugged rock walls slanted back toward the top, with a rocky floor that went gradually up. Then, at the end, a solid flat and very high rock face with no way out.

There was something else that couldn't be seen as you approached the canyon. In fact, you had to cross it to enter the canyon. It was a rocky gully that ran parallel to the mountains. It was shallow in front of the canyon, but it became deeper as it went north. Jack thought it looked like some past earthquake had just split the rock and it went as far as he could see. Now it served to channel the runoff from the occasional rains. If you traveled north down in the gully and you lead your horse, you wouldn't be seen.

Neither alternative appealed to Jack. They could be trapped in a boxed canyon or go down a gully where riders could catch you from above and shoot you down.

Dan and Chota were standing in the canyon entrance holding their horses. Jack slipped off the back of his horse then helped Fawn off Chilco. He went through the gully and up to his friends. He tried not to show his pessimism. "So, what now, Chota?" he asked flatly.

"We walk horses. I show you." Chota lead his horse into the box canyon and the others followed. It was an eerie place, dark with jagged rock walls that went up so high that it made them feel small. The floor was uneven, layers of gray flat rocks. Then up ahead, it simply stopped.

There were some soft murmurs of discontent from Dan's lips. Fawn and Jack just looked around and said nothing. About three quarters of the way in, Chota stopped. The canyon opened up some there. The first part had been wide enough for two horses to walk side-by-side, with little room to spare. Here it was three times that size. Ahead, it tapered back down to a narrow passage again before it stopped at the rock face.

Chota motioned to the right and stated, "This is it."

Dan couldn't stand it anymore. "Jack, we're trapped like rats in here! Even if we can hold them off for a while, they'll get us sooner or later!"

Jack saw the panic in Dan's face, but Chota was smiling. He walked over to the canyon wall and put his hands on a large flat layer of rock that was a little taller than he was and as wide as his outstretched arms. It was about the thickness of an adobe brick, was rounded at the bottom, and stood flat against the canyon wall. It butted against a similar looking layer of rock on the left. Chota rolled it to the right. There before them, was the entrance to a cave or cavern. The opening was big enough to allow a fair-sized horse through, but it became larger right away. Mouths were open, but no words were spoken.

They were stunned, but lost little time coaxing the horses through the entryway. Once all were inside, Chota picked up a couple of torches that were leaning against the rugged rock wall and lit them. He handed Dan and Jack each one of the two foot long straw-bound torches, walked back, and rolled the stone door closed.

The torches helped but you couldn't see too far. Chota came back to lead the way. There were several of the same type of torches placed along the wall. He took another, lit it, and then went deeper inside the cavern.

At first, Jack was reminded of mine shafts he'd been in before. But the farther they went in, the bigger it got. Before long, the ever larger shaft made a right turn. Then it opened up to what might be described as a large room. It was the same dark rugged-looking rock they'd seen the whole way, but it wasn't just a cavern. It was big. Jack calculated that the entire Longhorn Saloon would fit inside. The torch light made estimating depth and height difficult, but it was definitely impressive. There was no question of what it was used for. It was a storage room. Along the walls were rows of pots, baskets, and wooden shelves. Jack had heard of Indian tribes keeping corn, flour, grains, skins and anything else perishable in caverns. It's cool and dry there, kind of like a farmer's cellar.

What he hadn't heard of before, was keeping livestock in a place like this. But there, at the far end of this cavern was a corral with a water trough and bins of grass and grain just to the left of it.

The corral was made of mequite wood and fastened together with leather straps. It was large enough to accommodate the five horses. There were holes that were cut at an angle, spaced along the rock wall. Chota placed his torch in one of the holes. Then he took Dan and Jack's torches and put them in other holes, a ways apart. This gave a fairly even spread of light. As they brought the horses inside, Dan and Jack got busy taking the bridles, saddles, and packs off. These animals needed some rest, food, and water.

Chota's safe place had come as quite a surprise. As they went into this strange place, they had found themselves peering through the dimly lit passage with quiet fascination. There was also a sense of relief; Barlow's men would not find them here. These things were felt, but didn't really need to be said.

Understandably, Dan felt kind of bad for doubting Chota. "You sure came through, Chota." He smiled from behind a pack horse he was unloading and looked around the cavern. "This is the best dang hideout I ever heard of, partner."

"You help me. I must help you. It is only right," he answered and then started walking away from the corral.

"We all owe you for this, Chota," Jack added, he was pulling the saddle off Chilco. "How long will we be here?"

Chota looked over his shoulder, "I go find that out now." He continued to walk toward a recessed area of the cavern wall about a dozen steps from the corral. There, they could see what was a similar flat rock rounded at the bottom like at the entrance to the cavern. He rolled it to the right and stepped in.

They couldn't see far behind him, but just behind his feet was a flickering of light. As he turned around, his face seemed tense. He rolled the stone closed. They waited.

Chapter Eight
Spirit Feather

Chota had disappeared behind the stone over two hours ago. It seemed much longer than that. What might be behind that stone had been the focus of thought and discussion for Fawn, Jack, and Dan. There was even the temptation to move the stone themselves. Of course they didn't, they were honorable people. They simply had to wait.

During that period, Jack's mind turned to Barlow's men. By now they must have discovered that the canyon was both boxed and empty. At that point they probably figured that their quarry had escaped into the rocky gully. Jack smiled to himself as he envisioned them rushing to try to catch up, into the night. They'd come a long way fast for nothing.

The stone finally did open, but Chota wasn't

alone. Following behind him was another very pale Indian man. His clothes were made of deer skin, his hair came to his shoulders. He wore several ornate turquoise necklaces. His tan leather headband carried two feathers at the back forming a *V*.

Chota had always given the impression of a humble and simple man, Jack thought. This man, though, seemed self-assured and tough.

Jack had been casually leaning against the corral gate. Fawn and Dan were on his right. When Chota and his companion emerged from the stone doorway, there was one of those moments when Jack just wasn't sure who should approach whom. During that slight hesitation on Jack's part, as he wondered what was polite formality, Chota's companion walked briskly up to Jack and looked him up and down. He stared into Jack's eyes, turned to Chota, and said something to him in their language. He looked back at Jack and gave one defiant nod and crossed his arms.

"He want see you use guns but no shoot," Chota said apologetically. "He not believe me."

Jack moved away from the corral a little. He was about one step from the doubter. It was important that this man see some speed and flash, Jack thought. He didn't want to let Chota down. So he began a little show. He first did his famous quick draw. It was so fast, as usual, that neither of the men before him or any of the others actually saw it.

The Indian's eyes blinked as two colts just appeared, pointed at his face. Then Jack did the twirling routine. He'd spin them one way, then the other. Then in various directions. Next came the tossing routine. He'd throw the spinning guns up in the air and then catch them while maintaining the spin. Next he'd do the same thing, but toss them so they'd cross and he caught them with the opposite hands. He finally spun them back into their holsters, hoping that he had lived up to what Chota had said about him. It was hard to tell, though, his face showed little expression. Fawn and Dan seemed suitably impressed, both were grinning. Fawn was a bit giddy and was bouncing up and down on her toes while clapping in a quiet and petite manner.

After a few moments, the Indian man gave Jack a grudging nod, turned and walked past Fawn and Dan. He only seemed to give them token notice before giving the horses and supplies a more careful study. He came back to Chota and seemed to be having a rather serious conversation with him, judging from the look on Chota's face in response. When they concluded, Chota walked up to Jack, his expression was solemn. He looked at Jack and then motioned toward the other Indian with his eyes. "He is Tenkee, the chief's son. I tell him about you. I tell what you did for me and girl. He thinks you are good man, but is angry I bring you here."

"What is this place?" Jack had many questions, but Chota raised his left hand before he could go on.

"You must trust and show trust, so please no ask questions." He looked at Dan and Fawn. "I know this is hard thing. You must all come with me and leave weapons here." He turned back to Jack and saw a surprised and doubtful look on his face. "Please Jack, it is only way!"

Jack liked Chota and he was grateful for him leading them to this place, whatever it was. But Chota asked a lot. Going into the unknown without any weapons seemed very foolish. Yet Chota himself seemed to be in trouble just from their presence there. Jack found himself looking over at Dan who was equally perplexed. Then Jack smiled at Fawn, sighed, and unfastened his gun belt. Dan followed suit. They each handed their weapons and knives to Chota, who placed them with the supplies commandeered from the miners. Chota looked to Tenkee and they exchanged nods.

Tenkee went back through the stone doorway. Chota went to his saddlebag and took out the medicine he'd gotten in Tucson. He then headed for the same doorway while motioning for the others to come too.

Just beyond the entrance, it became wider. Chota waited just inside and the others passed by him, then he rolled the stone door closed.

It was like another room, but not nearly so large. They could see this well enough from the yellow glowing light that eminated from a round hole in the middle of the floor. There were also sounds coming through that hole, and the smell of smoke. There was a wooden ladder resting against the left side of the hole. Tenkee began climbing down.

It was Jack's turn next on the ladder, followed by Fawn, Dan and finally Chota. The hole was the entrance to another cavern. They descended from the top or roof of the cavern and along one of its walls. The ladder was quite long. Jack looked down and could see that the base of the ladder was on a stone and masonry block platform built into the cavern wall. The platform was about halfway up the wall. Another, equally long, ladder went from the cavern floor to that block platform. The cavern was lit by dozens of fires, so visibility was very good.

As Jack descended, he was astounded by what began to appear. When he reached the platform where he would have to change ladders, he stopped. He stood on the platform and turned to take it all in. It was a truly enormous cavern, but much more than that, it was actually an underground city. Built into the cavern walls was a massive complex of multi-level stone and adobe structures. They ranged from two and all the way up to five stories, depending on the shape and height of the cavern walls at various points. There was a wide courtyard between the dwellings that lined the walls. In the center of the courtyard was a large red clay fountain. Beyond the fountain was what looked like an altar. There were people everywhere. Children were at play, while men and women talked, worked and laughed. Familiar sights in a strange setting.

Fawn stepped off the ladder and joined Jack on the platform. She took a long slow sweep of the city. "Do you know who these people are?"

Jack simply shook his head.

"I've read about this." She continued to look with fascination. "The Navajos' call them Anasazi, which means 'Ancient Ones'." She looked up at Jack. "Anasazi were the cliff dwellers that built stone and adobe homes like these, but they disappeared hundreds of years ago. All anyone really knows about them is from the cities they left behind in canyons and the legends."

As Jack considered how and why these people came to live in this subterranean world, he noticed that Tenkee had now reached the courtyard and was looking up at him. It seemed clear, Jack thought, that Tenkee expected them to join him right away.

Dan was now on the platform and as he stared out at the city, he appeared speechless. Jack knew the feeling. Somehow words don't come easy when you come across a place so unexpected, so unimaginable.

Jack stepped onto the ladder that lead to the

courtyard and gave the others a little signal with his right hand to follow.

When they all reached the courtyard, Tenkee impatiently turned and walked ahead. He went around the fountain and stopped at the foot of the altar. While they followed Tenkee, all eyes of the population seemed to be on them. Not surprising, Jack considered, it must be a long time between visitors here.

Jack noticed some things as he walked along. The women wore a rather short and plain alabaster-colored dress that went over one shoulder and looked to be made of cotton. Many were adorned with simple turquoise jewelry. Their long hair was braided with bands highlighted with more turquoise. Jack preferred a woman's hair long and loose like Fawn's.

Most of the men, that Jack could see, were wearing pants of the same cotton material that stopped just below their knees. Some had on a deerskin vest. Some wore nothing on top. Like Tenkee, their hair came to their shoulders. The scant clothing made sense to Jack, for there was something else that he had noticed. The climate was warm and humid. He wondered what the water source was.

Tenkee seemed to be waiting for something or someone at the altar. Jack gave the altar a passing glance. It was a simple rectangular structure made of stone and mortar. It was much wider than it was tall. In fact, the top only reached his eye level. A series of stone steps led to the top.

There was tension felt as they waited there. What were they waiting for? What was the altar for? Jack could see that Fawn and Dan were nervous. His mind flashed on a scene of Aztec sacrifice he had read about, but dismissed it. Chota would not have brought them there for anything like that. His attention went back to the people of the city. They were pale like Chota, and seemed as fascinated with him as he was with them. All work had momentarily stopped as they watched the strangers.

The buildings, although all connected, were terraced back as they went up. The roof of one home was the patio of the one above it. There were ladders leaning against most of the buildings. Apparently, there were no internal stairs. As Jack looked up, he noted that the structures were four stories high where he stood. Although the homes were different sizes and shapes, they each had one rectangular window. In several of the windows were the faces of children. There were also many children playing in the courtyard, but keeping a distance from the strangers. Jack thought they acted as happy as any other youngsters. They wore a similar, but, of course, smaller version of their parents' clothes. But they were mostly barefoot, where the adults were wearing sandals, that Jack guessed were made of yucca.

Jack looked past the altar, trying to see just how far the cavern went. He was amazed by its size. There were fires going inside many of the homes. Some women also cooked on their patios. The flames reflected off the brown stone and red masonry. The entire city basked in a reddish orange glow. The light grew dimmer in the distance so judging length was impossible from where he was. Nevertheless, it was obvious by the number of dwellings, that hundreds of people could live in this place.

Out of the shadows, from that distant part of the city where the light was dim, emerged two men. As they came into the light, Jack saw that they dressed very much like Tenkee. Their deerskin pants and long sleeve shirts were decorated with leather stitching of bird feathers. They had turquoise necklaces like Tenkee, but the smaller man on the right had three feathers carried at the back of his head by a leather headband. The older and larger man was adorned with four feathers. It seemed evident to Jack that their attire spoke of some form of authority and that the feathers probably indicated rank or position.

When they approached the altar, Chota went to greet them. Jack watched them as they stopped a few paces from him. The words spoken, of course, meant nothing to Jack. They seemed cordial enough, though. The meeting ended with Chota handing the medicine to the smaller man, who then turned and walked back from where he came. Chota walked back to Jack and company with the large man just behind him. Chota motioned for them to move aside a little as the large man walked in front of them and made his way up the altar steps.

Chota glanced up at the man atop the altar and then back to his friends. "He is Tecanay. He is chief of our people," his eyes drifted a bit, right and left. "People here not used to outsiders. Some are scared, some are angry you come here. Tecanay tell people about you. Why you are here. Then he want to talk to you."

The chief stood on the altar and his voice echoed throughout the cavern city as he spoke. While his people gathered and listened, Chota went over to Fawn and talked to her quietly. Their little meeting ended with Fawn giving him a nod. Tecanay concluded his oratory at the same time. He went to the center of the altar and started down steps that Jack had not seen. The top of the altar was just about at Jack's eye level. The surface was made of dark stones that effectively hid the stairwell from his angle of sight.

Jack found himself thinking that surprises would probably continue in this place.

Tenkee had been standing quietly, off to one side, with his arms crossed. As Tecanay descended,

Tenkee climbed the altar steps and followed his father.

Fawn came up to Jack, getting his attention, "I've been talking to Chota. He is quite at home with the Papago language, but he knows his English is limited. So when the chief talks to us, Chota will tell it to me in Papago and I'll give it to you and Dan in English." She smiled up at him.

"It should work out fine." Jack nodded, "Did he say anything else?"

"Just that they have a problem with rickets here, especially with the children. You know they get no sunlight down here. And the chief's mother has severe headaches. That was the medicine man that he gave the medicine to."

"What did Chota get for her headaches?"

"Laudanum," she stated with disapproval in her voice.

Jack knew full well the addictive properties of the opium-derived tonic. He also knew it was very expensive and difficult to obtain. Not so for the fish oil and calcium used to treat rickets. It was just a long trip into Tucson for it.

Chota ascended the altar stairs, turned a little and gave a tilt of his head indicating for them to follow. He went to the center of the altar and started down the stairwell and noted that they were indeed, right behind him. Jack went down next, then Fawn and Dan.

It was a narrow stairwell that descended at a steep angle. The light was kind of dim going down the claustrophobic stair corridor. But at the bottom, it opened to a well-lit circular room. Jack noted that the roof was just high enough to clear his head. He figured the place could accommodate no more than a dozen people. Not that big, but he knew it took a lot of time and work for them to cut this out of the stone.

There were small blankets placed evenly around the periphery of the chamber floor. In the center was placed a large flat mat made of wicker. There were several torches set in angled holes drilled into the walls. All were lit.

Tenkee and Tecanay were sitting with their legs crossed on two of the small blankets directly across from the stairwell entrance.

Chota went around and sat on Tecanay's left. At the entrance, Fawn stood between Jack and Dan. After a moment's study, she looked up at Jack. "I know about this from reading about the Anasazi. It's called a 'kiva'. It's a ceremonial chamber. They use it for important meetings and spiritual services."

"What about grub? Is that served here?" Dan held his belly.

Jack gave Dan a wry smile and shook his head.

"I'm sorry, Jack, I just ain't used to going this long without vittles."

Chota spoke up from where he sat, ending Dan's

hunger complaints, "Fawn, come sit by me. Come Jack, Dan. Chief talk now!"

They complied. They sat to Chota's left. First Fawn, then Jack and Dan.

The chief began speaking. Not to anyone in particular, but rather like he was reciting a memorized text. He looked at no one. His eyes seemed to go up and down as he spoke, sometimes he closed them.

Chota would listen for a while, then whisper in Fawn's ear. When he stopped, she relayed the words to Jack and Dan in English. She spoke quietly, so Jack and Dan leaned into her, to hear her words above the chief's.

"There was a time that our people lived far from here in a red canyon," her translation began. "The city was built in the canyon walls, much like here, but it was much bigger. There were many more of us, then. We lived in peace and thrived. The game and our crops were plentiful. We traded with other tribes, and we were happy. So it was for many generations. Then, the war tribe came from the north and then to our city. They were called Apache. They would steal our food, our women, our children. But our people, our city survived. We went on in spite of the Apache raids. But then the rains stopped for many seasons. It was so dry that the crops failed. There was little food and the Apache would try to steal even that.

Our men had to go farther and farther to hunt. If

the Apache found them, they would steal their game, and sometimes kill the men."

Jack could see that translating all this was not easy for Fawn. The same could be said for Chota. They were doing their best to keep up. The chief paused for a moment. Maybe he did so to catch his breath, or maybe he sensed that Chota and Fawn were working pretty hard. It didn't last long, though, since he began again. So did his interpreters.

"One day, three of our hunters came to a mountain. They had killed many rabbits, but were being chased by a band of Apaches. They ran into a canyon to hide. One of the men saw a hawk's feather by his feet. Hawks are from the Spirit World, and he knew a hawk's feather was a sign. He picked up the feather and let it rest in the palm of his hand. He walked along the canyon looking at the feather. Then the feather raised up and then came down in a dark hole. That is how this place was found. That is why our city is called 'Spirit Feather'."

Jack's first thought was that it was probably a gust of wind that blew that feather into the canyon's entrance. On second thought, he decided, who's to say what forces are at work. It would be arrogant of him to dismiss other people's beliefs.

Tecanay's story and its translation went on. "Since that day, our whole tribe came to live here. We built a city and we have been safe here." Tecanay, then looked toward Jack and his words seemed more personal. "We have remained safe here all these generations because the outside world does not know about this place, or about us. We hunt at night so we can't be seen. We only have fires at night. There are holes and cracks high in the cavern where smoke escapes. It could be seen during the day. There are only a few men allowed to leave our city, Chota is one of them. When they go to bring back supplies and food, they don't go straight to the Papago tribe. They stay hidden in the gully you saw outside the canyon until they are far from here. They also return in the gully so no one is led here." Tecanay looked to his right at his son. Tenkee had been quiet throughout his father's speech, but his expression left little doubt of his displeasure. Tecanay turned back to his guests. "We understand why Chota had to bring you here. We don't blame him or any of you. But many, like my son, are angry and scared. They are afraid of the outside world and they don't trust you. They don't want you here, but we can't let you leave."

Tenkee was nodding like this was the one part of what his father had said that he wanted to hear. There were concerned faces on Dan and Fawn. Jack was calm as always. He raised his left hand a little, as if asking permission to speak in school. He smiled a little to reassure Fawn. "May I talk to the chief?"

Chota relayed the question and Tecanay nodded.

"You must know this about us. We are capable of doing things for your people that no one in your tribe can. Your mother needs medicine, we can get it for her. We can bring tools that will make cutting rock much easier." Jack then smiled at Fawn. "And she can teach your children many things." Jack found himself looking straight into Tecanay's eyes. "Chota told you about us. I think you know that you can trust us."

Tecanay took a deep breath and nodded. "I believe you can be trusted, but that is not enough. Many say not to trust you. We would have to know for certain that you can be trusted. Our survival depends on it. How can we be that certain?"

Tenkee stood up abruptly. Jack sensed he was issuing a challenge. "Qualtari!," he turned to his father and repeated it. "Qualtari!"

Tecanay looked long and hard at his son, as though he was trying to make an important decision. His eyes moved back to Jack. He had a look of resolve on his face. "You will sleep in the kiva tonight. No one will bother you in here. I will have food brought to you. Tomorrow, you will make decision. You will either become one of us, or you will face Qualtari." Tecanay could see the questions on his guests' faces. He raised his right hand to avoid further discussion. "All will be explained later. Now you rest."

With those words, he got up and left the kiva with Tenkee and Chota following.

Chota's face showed worry, not helping the confusion of those remaining. The food arrived as promised, along with three thick blankets, carried in by two older women. The women laid out the bowls and baskets containing dinner on the wicker mat in the center of the kiva. They stayed until the meal was finished. What remained was then cleared away along with the withdrawal of the two women.

Jack was amused by how quickly Dan slid beneath a blanket and drifted off to sleep. Fawn was only a few feet away and had her blanket folded behind her as she leaned back against the wall. She seemed in deep thought.

He sat beside her against the wall, looked her way, and gave a fond smile. "So, what do you think about all this?"

"I don't know what to think. This is a fascinating place, but what's all this about Qualtari?"

"Hard to say. Didn't make much sense to me either. But I wouldn't worry about it." He shook his head. "To be honest, I'm more curious than anything else."

"Well, we can't all be as brave as you are. I'm worried."

"Don't be, it doesn't help. And I think you're very brave. You got me out of a tight spot back there with Barlow's men. That was a brave thing to do."

"I wasn't brave. I was scared."

"But still, you did it. I call that brave. How'd you manage that?"

"I just had to." She said it as if it were a matter of fact.

"Because we helped you with the miners?"

"That's part of it." She seemed reluctant to say more.

He gave a prompting gesture with his eyebrows.

"Well, I'm Papago and we sense things. We can tell about people . . . I know what kind of man you are."

"Really? What do you know about me?" He smiled, not taking it too serious.

"I know you're honest and courageous and what the Mexicans call simpatico."

He shrugged awkwardly, showing that he was slightly embarrassed. "So, that's why you went back for me?"

"No." She looked away shyly.

"Then why?"

She hesitated before answering. Then she looked directly into his eyes. "I've seen how you look at me." Her eyes drifted down for a moment, then flashed back to his. "I went back because I know how you feel about me."

Jack swallowed noticably. "You sensed that because you're Papago?"

She shook her head. "Because I'm a woman."

There was an awkward pause, a moment of lingering silence. Jack found himself swallowing again. “And what else do you know about me?”

“Well, I know you want to kiss me.” There was a slight tremor in her voice.

He looked into her eyes and they seemed to captivate him. He felt something that was new to him. The long black hair, her charming face and those eyes. They were almost intoxicating. He was surprised that this lovely girl could have such an affect on him.

Jack wasn’t exactly unfamiliar with the charms of a woman. Yet, this small, beautiful and very direct girl was like no other. It was obvious that all the qualities she had said of him, were equally true of her.

He found himself being drawn closer to her. Their lips met, he put his hands around her waist and pulled her close.

Chapter Nine
Qualtari

Footsteps on the stairs woke Jack from a restless night's sleep. He watched as Chota led two older women who were carrying breakfast to the mat at the center of the kiva. They spread out a simple array of beans, corn, and some fried bread. It was like the previous night's dinner, minus the portion of rabbit. Once served, the women made a quiet exit.

Only one torch was left burning during the night. Chota went around and relit the others.

By this time, Dan and Fawn were also awake. They and Jack moved up to the mat with the food. Dan could not help but notice that something had changed between his partner and Fawn. They had been exchanging fond glances and were not very good at concealing their feelings. Chota then joined them, sitting with his legs crossed, on the opposite side.

Fawn passed out a bowl and wooden spoon to each of the men. They then began taking what they wanted from the larger red clay bowls.

It was a time of silent anticipation. It seemed obvious that Chota was there on behalf of the chief. They were all puzzled by the chief's parting statements and had more than a few questions. However, they were content to begin eating and wait for Chota to initiate conversation.

He had the same worried look he wore the previous night. He put down the bowl after a couple of bites and looked up at his friends. "Below our city, there is a river," he saw their eyes grow wider and they also put down their bowls. He definitely had their attention, so he continued. "Without water from river, we could not live here. But there is danger in river. Behind river wall, lives Qualtari." He now noticed their eyes narrow to a puzzled expression. "For as long as our people lived here, we pray to Qualtari. We give him ceremonial offerings. For all that time, he stay on his side of wall, we live in peace."

Jack didn't like to interupt Chota, but he had to ask, "What is Qualtari?"

"Qualtari mean Demon of River."

"Has anyone seen this demon?" Jack tried not to show too much scepticism.

"Many men try. They swim under river wall to face Qualtari. They never come back."

Confusion remained with Jack. "So, how do you know that Qualtari is even there?"

"He is there. When he moves, we feel ground and river shake. And we hear him. He has voice of demon."

"And the chief wants me to face the demon?"

"There is legend of our people. Legend says, a man one day face Qualtari, and will free us of him. This man have trust of all tribe."

Jack nodded, "So, the only way we're free to leave this place is for me to take on Qualtari!"

Chota nodded back.

"And no one ever comes back?"

Chota shook his head grimly.

Jack could see concern and doubt in Dan and Fawn's faces. He figured Dan would understand that he really had no choice in the matter. Fawn, on the other hand, might consider it too risky. Even Jack felt like he was going blindly into the unknown. It was, however, his nature to take risks. He found himself smiling at Fawn, partly to reassure her, partly because he had strong feelings for her.

She managed to briefly retain a little smile and then a frown appeared. "You're going to do this, aren't you?"

"It's the only way we can leave this place, at least without having to fight the whole tribe."

"Is that the only reason, because I don't want you to do this for me. I could live anywhere if you were there too." Her face blushed with the last few words and she looked away for a moment.

Jack noticed Dan facing him out of the corner of his eye. He seemed to act a little uncomfortable and turned away. Jack leaned closer to Fawn, and spoke softly, "I feel the same way, Fawn, but try to understand. I have to do this."

"I think you just can't resist a challenge."

"I'm afraid you're probably right."

She lowered her eyebrows and took his hand, "Alright, I guess I can't expect you to suddenly become cautious. But promise to come back to me!"

Jack pulled her close and whispered in her ear, "I promise, Fawn, nothing can keep us apart."

They fell into an embrace, much to the embarrassment of Dan and Chota.

About half an hour later, with breakfast and the kiva behind them, they walked down to the courtyard. Chota led them in the direction from which the chief and medicine man first appeared. It was darker than it was the previous night. All fires were out. The only light came from shafts of light emanating from a variety of holes and cracks above, that found their way through the rock to the outside.

There were still quite a number of people moving

about in the dim light. Soon, though, most would be asleep in this upside-down world, where life's activity is done at night so as not to bring attention to themselves.

Fawn's attention was on a particular woman who was finishing up some leather work. Fawn excused herself and went to see the woman's craft.

Jack and Dan viewed the complex of tiered structures and watched the movement of people with interest. Dan had more than a little interest in a couple of women standing nearby in their customary scant dresses. He nudged Jack and gave a tilt of the head in their direction. "Maybe it wouldn't be so bad living down here, Jack." The sly grin seemed out of character to Jack.

"I don't think you're really serious about settling down here, Dan. Now, this wouldn't have anything to do with Qualtari, would it?"

"Yup! I ain't got a good feeling about this, Jack. I mean, if you were facing any man, heck, any five men, I wouldn't think twice about it! But how can you go up against this demon?"

"Come on Dan, do you really think there's a demon down there? Do you actually think there is such a thing as a demon?"

"Well, I bet you wouldn't have believed there was such a thing as a lost tribe in an underground city? And, how about an underground river? After what we've come across down here, I don't think we can be too dang sure about anything."

Jack could see how sincere Dan was being, but he couldn't help giving him an incredulous look.

Just ahead, there was a hole in the courtyard floor. It was jagged and oval shaped. There was a wide ladder protruding on the far side.

Chota headed toward the jagged hole, so Jack and Dan went to follow. After only a couple of steps, they started feeling vibration in the floor. Then, coming from the hole, was a deep menacing moan. It grew louder and after, maybe fifteen seconds, suddenly stopped. It was an eerily frightening sound.

Fawn came running up to Jack. "What was that?" her voice trembled.

"Qualtari." Chota stated soberly, while looking down the hole. Chota then turned to his friends. "He's angry today!"

While Jack was receiving worried stares from Fawn and Dan, Tenkee and Tecanay approached from behind. They came from one of the larger dwellings across the courtyard. Tenkee watched as his father spoke to Jack through Chota. "The chief want know if you will face Qualtari!"

Jack gave a nod and Fawn looked away, shaking her head.

"He say you must face Qualtari alone. He say

you must have no weapons. It is part of legend, it must be this way."

Jack shrugged and then gave another nod. This seemed to satisfy Tenkee, as they each offered Jack a hand to shake. With that, Chota went to the ladder and started down.

Jack knew he was expected to follow, but found himself, instead focused on Fawn, who was still looking away. He put his hand on her shoulder.

She slowly turned. Her eyes were a little misty. They looked at one another for a moment and then fell into each other's arms. It ended in a long kiss.

As Jack felt her in his arms, he then felt her hand slide toward his. As they looked into each other's eyes, she passed a knife, which she had palmed, into his hand. It was when they stepped apart that Jack noticed her necklace was gone. She had done a little trading with the woman who was doing the leather work.

Jack gave her one last smile and handed her his Stetson. "I'll be back for that." He then gave Dan a little slap on the back and followed Chota down the ladder. Jack kept the knife concealed in his hand until he was part way down the ladder, then slipped the knife, unnoticed, into his right pants pocket.

Two flickering torches were burning below. They were resting at an angle, in the river wall.

Chota had just lit them as Jack stepped off the fifteen foot ladder. Two torches were enough to see the length of the river within what was another, although much smaller, cavern.

The cavern looked a lot like a railroad tunnel that had been sealed on each end. Probably thirty paces would cover its length. The water went all the way to the left wall. On the right side, the side with the ladder, was a narrow walkway that spanned the length of the cavern. A rock face came down and sealed off both ends below the waterline.

The water had a slight current. It went in the direction away from the ladder. So, although it couldn't be seen from above, there had to be passages on both ends, below the surface, letting the water flow through the cavern.

As Jack stepped onto the narrow walkway, Chota commented, "Our men spend much time here. They carry water to fountain above. Much work every day."

"They're not afraid of Qualtari?"

Chota pointed to a few baskets behind him sitting on the walkway. "In baskets, is food for Qualtari." He motioned toward the far end of the river. "When Qualtari call us, we give offerings. We pour grain into water for him, down where river ends. I did this before you come down. For this, Qualtari stay on other side of wall. We know this."

That sort of logic made little sense to Jack. But he couldn't dismiss or explain what he had felt and heard. For most people, unknown danger would cause feelings of uneasy tension and fear. Jack, in contrast, was filled with curiosity.

Chota stepped around the baskets and lead Jack to the river's end. He put his hand on the wall that closed off the cavern. "You must swim down under wall to find Qualtari." He had difficulty looking him in the eyes. His expression was troubled. "You not have to face Qualtari, this not bad place to live."

Jack put his hand on Chota's shoulder. "I have to do this. I think you understand that."

Chota nodded reluctantly and stepped around him. He looked down and headed for the ladder. It seemed that he couldn't even look at Jack, let alone speak to him. It wasn't an easy moment for either man.

Jack finally called to him when he was halfway up the ladder, "Look after Fawn for me!"

Chota continued up the ladder and simply gave another nod.

Jack couldn't dwell on other's concerns and doubts. It was always his clear thinking and self-confidence that allowed him to do his best. He possessed amazing speed and skill with weapons, but that wasn't enough. A man that is cool under pressure always has an edge. He knew that he had to think only of the obstacles before him. Then he would find a way to resolve them as they became known to him. Besides his ability to think and act rationally in dangerous situations, he believed he had a couple of advantages going in. Jack was a powerful man and was very fit. He had no fear of water and could handle darkness equally well.

Jack pulled his boots off to get ready for an exploratory dive. He always carried an emergency knife in his right boot. He put that knife in his left pants pocket. *A knife in each pocket doesn't equal a gun, but it's not bad,* he mused. Jack dropped down into the water. It was surprisingly warm. His plan was simple enough. He had a pretty good feel for how long he could go on one breath. He figured that he would first make some test dives. He'd just poke around a little, remembering how long he had been down and try to sense what he was up against. He took several deep breaths to charge his lungs with oxygen. Then he took one more final gulp of air and went straight down, head first. He used the rugged rock wall surface to his advantage. Instead of using a lot of energy swimming down, he used the rocks to pull himself down. Like a rock climber scales a rock face, Jack used them to climb in reverse.

Within seconds, he was down ten feet. At that depth, he felt the passage open up. He even felt a mild current running into it. He pulled himself into the passage and felt around in all directions. The passage was extremely jagged and undulating.

Suddenly, in this total darkness, a recollection flashed into his mind. There could be air pockets in this passage. He remembered a story that he had once read. It was about a man in Minnesota, who fell through a weak spot in an ice covered lake. The man survived by finding air pockets beneath the rugged ice. He finally found another opening and climbed out. Jack reasoned that there could be air pockets in this passage too. Now, as he moved further into the passage his objective was to feel above him for a cavity to test this notion. The trouble was he was getting past the point in which he had promised himself to turn back. Just at that moment, where he started feeling he'd maybe gone too far, he reached up and felt his hand come out of the water. He fought off the panic that was engulfing him and kicked up into the cavity above him. It was as risky a thing as he'd ever done. He went up into the cavity in total darkness until his head suddenly popped out of the water.

He was desperate to breathe, but he still tested the air with a little taste. He tried a little more. It was stale, and pungent, but it was air.

For several minutes, he stayed up in the cavity, filling his lungs and thinking. In order to go on, he would have to find more air pockets. This seemed a reasonable gamble to Jack. The trick would be, that if he didn't find a new air pocket, he'd have to find his way back to this one. It would be too far to make it all the way back up to the cavern on one breath.

The thing he had to resolve was how to stay on a

straight course in total darkness. Jack didn't like the idea of turning back. While he pondered, he let his right hand drop down to his side. *That's my means of navigation,* he thought. *The current. As long as I go straight with the current, I can find my way back.*

Jack took a deep breath, pushed his way out of the cavity, and went further into the passage. He was careful to not only feel for another possible air pocket, but to also test the current with his open hand. It was difficult to judge distance as he made his way along, but after about forty seconds, he felt another cavity. He came up to find more of the very welcome stale air. His confidence was high. He rested a while and then continued. He moved along as before. It seemed like it was getting close to a minute with no air pocket. He was just about to turn back when he saw something.

Ahead of him, in the distance, was a glimmer of light. He instinctively picked up the pace. The light became closer and a little brighter, but he was still within the passage.

Jack was working pretty hard, kicking his feet and using a lot of energy. Just about the time that he was starting to doubt his chances, the passage seemed to open up. There was light above him and the water was very warm. He felt something moving beneath him.

Suddenly, he was being pushed straight up. He was being lifted up and out of the water and at the same instant, there was an incredibly loud and deep roar below him. Jack found himself being lifted out of the water and up into another huge cavern. He was lifted so fast and so high that he struck hard against the roof of the cavern. Fortunately, the cavern was lit enough that he was able to brace against the impact. He hit it with a thud. Jack then fell some twenty odd feet and splashed back into the water.

When he bobbed back up to the surface, Jack looked around and caught his breath. There were shafts of light streaming down from several holes in the jagged cavern roof. He turned a full circle in the water. He was floating in an underground lake. There was a ledge a little above the waterline a ways off to his right. He swam to it, and pulled himself out of the water.

He was banged up a bit. His right shoulder and hip took most of the impact and really hurt. His right hand was cut a little across the palm and bleeding, but he was alright. He looked out across the lake.

It was not possible to see the entire length of the lake. All the light was at his end. In the distance, the lake disappeared into darkness. It was fairly wide, he could see that far, and he seemed to be nearly midway between the cavern walls. He looked up where a number of jagged openings let the light in, high in the cavern's roof. That's where he wanted to go, up and out.

At that moment, however, he didn't know how he

was going to get there. He did know one thing for certain, he knew that Qualtari, in reality, was a geyser. It was a geyser that had frightened the Indians all those years. It was the same geyser that had just blasted Jack out of the lake. The source of heat for the geyser had to be very deep because although the blast from it was hot, it was tolerable.

During the next few moments, Jack studied the place more closely. It was the size and beauty that first drew his attention. The clear water shimmering under rays of light from above. The vertical brown and copper-colored walls that shined from a sporadic geyser's spray. And, looking straight up, the roof reminded Jack of a cathedral ceiling. The roof wasn't just rugged rock. There were rocky, upside down spires where the point faced downward. There were also several funnel-shaped cavities that reached high above and opened to the outside air. This, of course, was also how the light penetrated the cavern.

In the clear water, he could see some pretty good sized fish. It occurred to Jack that because of Qualtari, the Indians had been inadvertently feeding these fish.

As fascinating as Jack found the place, he turned his attention to his primary goal, escape. The walls were nearly vertical and slick from geyser eruptions. Also, Jack noted that there were plenty of cracks, crevasses and protrusions to aid in climbing. With two knives, he knew that he could work his way straight up. He could wedge a knife into a crack and use his powerful arms to pull himself up to the next one. The less frequent protruding rocks and crevasses could be utilized by his feet to stop and rest. He could scale the twenty odd feet of wall, alright, but, then came the overhang.

The actual cavern roof was another matter. There was a considerable span of rugged cavern roof to cross before he could begin ascending the funnel-shaped cavity that vented to the outside. Jack didn't like to use the word "impossible", but he wished there was another way. Time slipped away while Jack considered his options. There weren't many. No matter where he began climbing, he still had to face the overhang. The idea of going back was out of character. Even if he were to go back, it would be much harder than it was getting there. He'd be going against the current, and he wouldn't have the help of a lucky geyser blast to help him out.

Chapter Ten
No Way But Up

Jack sat on the ledge gazing across the lake. His eyes were drawn to a few bubbles coming to the surface a ways out. That was the point where he had first come up. He tried to judge where that was in relation to the cavern roof. Darn close to the funnel shaped vent, he figured.

Jack slipped back into the water and headed for the bubbles. He placed himself right in the center of the raising pool of bubbles and looked up. It was just a little to the left of that funnel. It seemed crazy, but he considered the odds were better than anything else. He found himself smiling and inwardly laughing at himself. Jack pulled the two knives out of his pockets and held them in each hand. He floated on his back, staying in the center of the bubbles and waited for the geyser.

He didn't have long to wait. The water began to rush up as though it was boiling. Jack tried to ride it out and maintain his position. He looked up to see if he was drifting off his mark while paddling his arms and feet in defense of the upward current. Then, with a suddenness that he couldn't prepare for, the geyser blew. With the blast, came the deafening roar. It was a deep shattering moan that was just as alarming as being blasted twenty some feet into a roof of jagged rocks.

The geyser hurled his body upward with more than enough force to reach the cavern roof. Jack had hoped to be able to use one of the knives for the first crucial hold in the rocks. If he saw a space between two rocks or even a crack, he thought he'd have a chance to plant a knife into it. That would be just the starting point for his escape.

It didn't happen that way. The force of the blast, not only carried him up, it also made him turn in midair. He ended up hitting the rocks facing down. His back took the brunt of the impact. He felt the wind forced out of his lungs. Pain shot across his back, while at the same time, his right temple glanced off of a flat rock. For a fraction of a second, darkness dulled his mind, but he held on to the knives. He came falling down face first into the water with a painful, slapping sound. The water was still churning with bubbles and he came up fast. His head broke through the water and he gasped for air.

He managed to slip the knives back into his pockets. Then he slowly made his way back to the ledge. He put his arms up on the ledge and breathed heavily for quite a while. It had all gone wrong.

It took some time before he felt good enough to pull himself all the way onto the ledge. The ledge wasn't very wide where he was. He was just able to lay on his left side and rest. His back was stiff and aching. His head throbbed. Blood ran down the right side of his face. His mind and vision were both blurred. Soon, he was asleep.

Jack didn't know how long he had slept, but he awoke with his senses clouded and staring up at the light reflecting off the cathedral-like roof. Briefly, he let his mind drift to Fawn and her charming face. But then, as his mind began to clear, he forced himself to stop. A difficult situation required undivided attention and a single-minded stubbornness. It would take all his physical and mental strength to escape the cavern. *A bit of luck too,* he thought.

The light coming into the cavern was still bright. He figured that there was still time for another try. He wasn't about to give up. He sat up again on the ledge. There were few parts of his body that didn't hurt. He waited.

Before very long, he saw the bubbles start to

foam to the surface. He slipped back into the water. Jack did as he had done earlier. Both knives were in his hands. He fought as before to stay in the center of the blast. It came with the same sudden fury and volume.

Jack was blasted up, but not straight up. He found himself to be going to the right. His body was turning too. This time, however, his feet were dropping down, he was nearly flying vertical. He was heading straight for the funnel-shaped cavity that he thought he'd have to work his way over to. It was a lucky break if he could manage to get a hold of something.

Jack had to resist the natural instinct to protect himself. He was heading fast and hard into the far side of the funnel wall. He had to focus on finding something to sink a knife into and not think about slamming into the rock.

At the last possible instant, he saw a horizontal crevice. He stabbed at it with his right hand with all his strength. At that same time he struck the wall, flat and hard. He had wedged the knife into the crevice, but as he bounced back from the impact, it loosened.

Jack's eyes were blinking from striking the wall, but he frantically looked for another knife hold. He reached up and drove the knife, carried in his left hand, deep into another gap between rocks. Just as he did so, the first knife slipped, but the left knife held. Jack let out a sigh. He clenched his teeth and pulled himself up with his left hand. He then worked the other blade into the same gap. For the time being, he let his arms go straight. He felt secure.

Before attempting the ascent, Jack paused to clear his head and assess what faced him. It was at least twenty feet up to the top, he estimated. The hardest part was at first, since he was in an upside down funnel. His feet would be dangling below until it tapered down small enough to use his feet against the sides. Even the opening at the top was an uncertainty. He couldn't be sure if he'd be able to squeeze through when he got there. He would worry about that when the time came.

There was one other thing that caught his eye, although it didn't affect the climb. About halfway up, he could see something reflecting light: a shiny line glinting between the rocks. He took a deep breath to prepare for the climb.

The two knives that Jack possessed were suitable for the task. The one he had kept in his boot was a throwing knife. The blade was rather short and very stiff. The one passed to him by Fawn was made for cutting leather. It was a little longer, still it too was plenty strong.

Jack pulled himself up until he was eye level with the knives. Above him and a little to the left, he saw a tiny space between two rocks. He carefully worked his left knife out and reached up to it. After driving the blade into the new crevice, he did the same with the right one. And so it went, slowly, carefully, and with growing fatigue.

Twenty minutes of exhausting effort brought him up to the point above the cone of the funnel. Now he was into the smaller, vertical shaft that went straight up. It became a little easier here. Although the shaft he found himself in was hardly uniform in size. Most of it was small enough that he could now use his back and feet.

Jack pushed against a rock protrusion with his foot so he could wedge himself against his back and take some strain off his hands and arms. The rock was slick from moisture and patches of dark green moss, so he couldn't completely relax his grip on the knives. He tried to relax a little for a few moments.

Above, he now noticed, was that glittering band that he had seen earlier. His curiosity was aroused. It would take a few more minutes to reach it. He continued his careful ascent.

Jack managed that part of the climb without drama. He wedged both blades into a convenient split in the rock, just above his new center of focus.

His eyes were now fixed on a yellow metallic stripe that angled up to his left. A vein of gold was certainly not expected during his attempt to escape. Now it consumed his attention. The seam of yellow metal was less than the length of his arm. It was about two fingers thick at the widest point, but varied along its length to barely the thickness of a shoelace. Although the gold would rightly be described as a vein, it wasn't continuous. There were sections and bits separated by rock.

Jack was surprised by his fascination with the shiny metal. Whether it was the gold's captivating beauty or the excitement of its discovery, somehow, he felt compelled to stop and extract a piece. There, within easy reach, was a piece about the diameter of a penny, but with one flat side.

There was enough rock around it that it looked like you could dig it out fairly easily. He put his escape on hold long enough to give it a try, reasoning that it wouldn't take long and was worth the risk.

There was a small protruding rock by Jack's right foot that jutted out a little. He used it to push himself up and back to brace himself firmly into position. He then pulled the right hand knife out of the crevice so he could start digging around the gold.

The rock was hard and the digging went slowly. In frustration, Jack found himself stabbing, twisting and rapidly levering with the knife. He was flicking pieces and chips of rock away all around what looked like a nugget. The deeper he dug, the more gold could be seen. It was surprising to find such a large chunk of gold.

Under different circumstances, this would have been a very welcome surprise. As it was, Jack was getting weary of the venture and was anxious to get on with the climb.

The light that shone down from above was a little dimmer now. Jack now knew that the sun was on its downward ark, still, he had no idea of how much time was left before the darkness came. He gritted his teeth and dug deeper. Jack McCall didn't like to fail at anything.

Finally, the nugget began to move just a bit, but unfortunately, it wouldn't come out. Just using his right hand wasn't working. Between the climbing and now all the digging, his right arm and wrist ached.

Something else occurred to him. If he pried too hard with the knife, the nugget would likely get away from him when it finally and suddenly did break free.

Jack felt solid enough in the position that he was in. His right foot was planted onto that protruding rock and his back was pressed hard up against the wall. If he used both hands, he could get this over with, he thought.

He released his grip on the knife, wedged above him. After switching the knife, he'd been digging with, into this left hand, the chipping away continued. Jack let his right hand hang relaxed to his side while this went on and soon, the aching subsided.

Time and patience was running out. The nugget would move a little, but no more than that. Jack remembered an old adage: If all else fails, try brute force. His right arm felt pretty good now. After returning the knife to his right hand, he forced it in behind the nugget. His left hand was held open-handed over the gold. After all this effort, he wasn't going to let it get away.

Jack braced himself, made a little grunting sound and pushed hard. He couldn't have seen what happened because his left hand was covering the nugget, but it didn't give way. It did, however, turn enough to make the knife slip. When the knife slipped out, Jack lurched forward and right. He mashed his knuckles into the rock and had to push down hard with his foot to right himself. There must have been a crack in that protruding rock, because the increased force caused the corner of the rock to suddenly break off. Jack's foot went with the broken rock and he started going straight down.

Instinctively and instantly, he brought his knees up and pushed out with his feet. Painfully, his feet, knees and back dragged against the narrow rugged shaft. This, as he hoped, caused a wedging affect and it slowed the fall a little. He only had ten feet before the funnel opened up and he'd be back in the water. Jack ignored the pain, locked his attention on spotting a gap in the rock and slammed the knife in.

The blade went in, but not as far as he hoped. He knew it could just as easily slip out.

Instantly, he grabbed onto his right hand with his left hand. It would take all his strength to stop the fall while keeping the knife perpendicular to the wall. If his wrists failed him and the knife tipped down, it would come right out and there wouldn't be another chance.

A deep agonizing groan echoed through the cavern. Jack was the very picture of pain. He had muscled against the speed and force of gravity and for the moment, had won. His face was red, with veins expanded around his forehead. His teeth were tightly clenched and sweat flowed into his eyes. As he tried to stay very still and catch his breath, he looked up. "What now?" he wondered.

Jack was still in the crouched position used to slow his descent. He dared not move. He had one overwhelming problem. How could he move up with only one knife? He had to do something quickly, this wasn't easy on his arms. They were at a ninety degree angle. Soon they'd start to shake.

Calculated risks were a way of life with Jack McCall. He took one then without hesitation. With reflexes and dexterity that few possess, he released his left hand's grip and went for his belt buckle. This put enormous strain on his right hand, wrist and arm. He didn't have much time. In one motion, he unhooked the buckle and pulled the belt free of his pant loops. He then put the buckle end in his mouth, reached down for the other end of the belt, and brought it up through the buckle. Just like a lasso, he flung the open end of the belt up. It was nearly six feet up to the knife he had left wedged into that crevice above the gold vein. All those rope tricks he did every day in the show would serve him well at that moment. He roped it easily the first try and none too soon. Just as the belt found its mark, his right wrist gave way and the blade slipped out.

Jack felt the belt slide inside his left hand when the weight of his body suddenly hit against his grip. He now found himself dangling from the belt and swinging from side-to-side. He still had a hold of the knife in his right hand. His grip on the belt was slipping. A couple more inches of belt and a couple more seconds would find him heading for the water.

With his customary speed, Jack put the knife blade into his mouth and then desperately reached up to grab the belt. He had to reach above his left hand, which meant, he had to actually pull himself up farther. As he did so, the last of the belt slipped through the fingers of his left hand. Frantically, he stretched out his right arm and just managed to clasp the very end of the belt. He then reached back up with his left hand. Now, with both hands around the belt, he let out a sigh.

For just a few moments, he hung there motionless. Then he took a deep breath through his nose and pulled himself up to eye level with his hands. From there, he climbed the rest of the way, hand over hand.

Once back up to the knife in the crevice, he took the knife from his mouth and wedged it back in the crevice, just right of the other one. He paused there, once again peering at the gold.

There was something different from when he last looked at the very uncooperative nugget. Just above the gold was a vertical crack, about the width of a knife blade, caused from his last nearly disastrous extraction effort, Jack figured.

After all the trouble this nugget had been, his first impulse was to simply let it go. However, that crack seemed tantalizing. *One more try,* he thought. A little smile grew and he found himself stating aloud, "I sure am stubborn!"

Jack brought his knees up to brace himself as best he could. He pulled out the right hand knife again and started driving it into that crack. He worked it in and moved it from side-to-side. Within minutes, a small chunk broke off. With that done, he was able to maneuver the nugget around until it loosened up. In less than five minutes, he had a sort of egg-shaped nugget between his fingers. He put the gold into his pocket and returned the knife to the crevice. The belt, still looped around the right hand knife handle, he simply slid over his left arm, out of his way. He felt some remorse for all the wasted time. He then, once again, began working his way up.

Less than thirty minutes of slow, exhausting effort brought Jack near the top. Fatigue now slowed his progress. Lack of food and water didn't help. His body had numerous cuts, bruises and scrapes. Sweat dripped into his eyes. Still, he continued. He pulled himself up within an arm's length of freedom. Light was fading fast now. The shaft itself was so tight, that it was claustrophobic. But this part of the shaft also had some advantages for Jack. There were a number of rock edges and grooves. Jack was now able to get hand and footholds. The knives were no longer necessary. He put both blades in his mouth, and then pushed, pulled and squirmed his way up to the top.

It was twilight when Jack's head finally emerged into the open air. There wasn't much to see. He was surrounded by a scattering of the same rocks he had been climbing through and some brush around and between the rocks. The last part of the shaft was really tight. He had to drop down a little, put his hands over his head and force his shoulders through. After that, he pushed down with his hands to hoist himself out.

He stood motionless for a few moments beside the open shaft. He let his hands hang to his side and felt some of the pain and stiffness fade. While appreciating the simple pleasure of standing on level ground, he slid the knives into his pockets and put on his belt. His overall feeling was one of relief. Now, he had to see just where he was.

Jack walked away from the shaft entrance and out beyond the rocks. He stood on a sandy plateau and peered into the shadowy landscape. There was still a glow in the west behind the distant mountains that gave the sky a dark purple tint. Between himself and the mountains, the desert floor stretched out in contrasts of black and gray. Just ahead, the plateau dropped down a little to a lower hillside. Below that and a little ways further out, he could see the boxed canyon.

Jack glanced back toward the rock and brush that hid the shaft entrance. It was well camouflaged. He was not surprised that no one before had discovered it. He studied it from where he stood so he could find it again later. He also took note of the position of the two spires. They were behind the rocks and much higher, as were the mountain crests they stood on. With these points logged into his memory, he was ready to begin his descent. The light grew ever dimmer, so he had to go down slowly and with care. Nevertheless, compared with what he'd just gone through, it was easy and not too far down.

Chapter Eleven
Conquering Hero

It was quite dark by the time Jack made his way into the boxed canyon. The moonless night made the stars all the brighter. Jack found himself gazing thoughtfully into the sky. Being under all those stars made him feel rather small. They also made him feel free.

Jack had left the show because he had missed his freedom. The experience he had just gone through was the price of freedom. He felt the chief and the Anasazi people would honor their word and he would have earned their trust and he'd be free to go. He wasn't quite so sure if it would apply to Dan and Fawn. He wasn't about to leave them behind.

As Jack walked the last few steps to the cavern's entrance, he thought of how he must appear.

Besides the pain he felt from head to toe, he knew he had to look bad. Torn clothes, bruised and bloody, it was not how people thought of Jack McCall. Jack was battered, fatigued and very hungry. He needed food, water, and rest, but what he wanted most, was to see Fawn.

He rolled the stone door open and felt his way along the corridor to the storage room. There was a single torch lit by the corral. Remembering that the Anasazi legend expected him to face Qualtari unarmed, he stashed the knives with his gear just to be safe. Then he headed for the village and Fawn.

The village was teaming with activity as Jack descended the two ladders to the courtyard. Jack's arrival went unnoticed until his last few steps down the ladder. Once he had been seen, the news seemed to spread quickly. Unexpectedly, as Jack stood on the courtyard floor and looked around, he was swarmed by jubilant people. They gathered around him, smiling and enthusiastic.

Soon, Chota came toward Jack wearing a wide grin. He cut through the crowd with Tecanay and Tenkee in tow. When Chota got close enough to him, Jack pulled the nugget out of his pocket and tossed it to his Indian friend. This, as Jack expected, stopped them in their tracks. They passed it around between the three of them with stunned expressions. Even down in this hidden city, they knew the significance of gold. Jack's interest was that it might further build their trust. He also knew, as they did, that the whole tribe would have an easier time of it now. Food, medicine, tools, nothing was beyond their grasp.

Jack certainly didn't feel like a conquering hero, yet, that was how the people acted. He enjoyed the reaction of Chota and company with the gold, but felt a little awkward about the adulation from the crowd. He wondered what they'd think when they found out that there was no demon.

Then, suddenly, none of that mattered. Jack's attention was drawn way to the back of the crowd. There, approaching with Dan, was Fawn. They both hurried through the crowd to each other's arms. Her eyes were red from worry. There were tears of relief flowing down her cheeks. He sensed that she had concern because of his appearance. He held her tight to reassure her that he was okay. Within his embrace, he felt her trembling slightly. She then lifted her head and looked up at him with tearful eyes. "I thought I'd lost you." The words trailed off with a little quiver of her lip.

He kissed her softly and then looked tenderly into her eyes. "You know, I had to come back to you."

"Because you promised?" her eyebrows raised slightly.

He nodded with a little smile.

"Because you love me?" she moved her head back defensively as she asked it.

He nodded again, but more slowly. He saw the light in her eyes, but somehow felt compelled to break the serious mood. "And one other reason," he stated.

She looked at him quizzically. "What's that?"

He gave her a boyish grin. "Well, you've got my hat."

She tried to look angry and then gave in to an impish smile. He pulled her closer and kissed her again.

Jack spent the next three days in the Anasazi city. He gave Tenkee and Tecanay the details of what he had encountered beyond the river walls, through Chota. They listened with fascination. The concept of a geyser was the only difficult thing to explain. It was also hard for them to accept that the long held belief of Qualtari simply wasn't true.

On Jack's suggestion, Tecanay ordered the making of a suitably long rope ladder in which to enter the lake. The three days it took the tribe to make it was just what he needed to heal and rest. It was a very pleasant time for Jack. He was able to spend time with Fawn and really get to know her. Dan seemed to have plenty of questions about this last experience and found the Qualtari story mighty interesting.

While Jack recovered from his last adventure, he came to appreciate the warm, happy people who lived there. He was no longer looked upon with suspicion or even as an outsider. Jack needed the wide-open western expanse to feel completely free. Still, he felt at home there now, and liked the idea of returning from time to time. He was sure that the tribe would need him as a go-between in the future, and that was fine with him.

When Fawn wasn't with Jack, she was with the children. She tirelessly played and looked after the smaller kids. Jack knew her dream was to teach. He wondered how receptive these people would be to that. They accepted her for the sweet and kind person that she was. Letting her watch over their children proved that. Teaching the ways of the outside world was another matter. Jack could see how that would scare them. As peaceful and harmonious as this underground city was, could they risk tantalizing young minds with visions of the world above? *Not likely*, he thought.

Still, Fawn was happy. There was little point in raising the question of teaching. He would, though, have to tell her he was leaving soon. Perhaps she knew already. She was very bright and seemed to be able to read him pretty well. Just the same, he would wait until the last moment to tell her. He hoped that she would understand. It was time to deal with Brad Barlow.

By the end of the third day, the rope ladder was finished. It was early morning when Jack led four young men up to the shaft entrance that he'd escaped from. They carried the ladder and a good stout pole. They looped the pole through the end of the rope ladder and then dropped the other end into the shaft. They fed the entire ladder into the shaft, while using the pole across the opening to support it. Three of the men then descended into the cavern as Jack and the other young man made sure the pole stayed in position. About a half hour later, they emerged from the shaft. They seemed delighted by what they had seen. They even managed to bring out a couple of large fish, speared with their knives.

Just as they started pulling the ladder back out, the geyser blew. The four young men jumped back, letting the rope fall back down. They had startled expressions. Jack's big smile seemed to reassure them and they finished removing the ladder.

When they returned to the village, Jack stood back a ways and watched as the men reported to the chief and his son. Soon Chota was summoned to the chief. After a little meeting, he walked over to Jack. "Tecanay want see you, Jack."

Jack nodded, and they headed toward the other side of the fountain where the chief and his son stood. The four young men left shortly before Jack and Chota's approach. Although it was morning above, it was late for those in the tribe and they were probably off to get some sleep. There were a few torches near the fountain still lit, but the light was dim.

Tecanay and Tenkee met Jack with outstretched hands. Jack gave each a firm handshake, then the chief spoke. "You have done well for our people," Chota interpreted. "We are grateful that spirits brought you here." Tecanay put his left hand on Jack's shoulder. "We hope you want stay with us." Chota translated while nodding in agreement.

Jack felt honored by the chief's words. He hoped Chota's translation of his own words would not offend. "I want to be a part of your people and I hope to be of help to them. But I have to travel beyond this place. I cannot, and Dan and Fawn cannot be here always. But we will be back, and we will guard your secrets. I think you know that you can trust us."

Tecanay nodded. "Yes, we trust you. You are always welcome here." Tecanay then turned to his son and held out his hand. Tenkee handed his father the gold nugget. Then Tecanay held the nugget before Jack. "Will you get money for gold? We cannot do this."

"You're right, men will kill for this or they'd follow you back here," Jack agreed. "I'll cash this in and open a bank account for Chota. That way, when he needs it, he can have money in town without carrying a lot around." Jack looked to his Indian friend. "Can you leave tomorrow?"

Chota nodded and then they all shook hands again.

With the meeting concluded, Jack walked around the kiva to the bottom level room that the chief let them stay in. It was rather dark inside, but he could still see Fawn sleeping sweetly on the left side. His mat was next to hers. Across on the right side, Dan slept restlessly while making little grunting sounds. Fawn and Dan seemed to adjust to the hours of sleep better than he had. The quiet darkness certainly helped, but Jack was wide awake, so he laid beside Fawn and put his hands behind his head.

Jack didn't mind helping the tribe. The timing, however, was bad. Jack was going into town to settle affairs with Brad Barlow and his men. He had hoped to have surprise on his side. Going into town and dealing with the assay office and the bank could alert Barlow. This wasn't going to make things any easier.

As Jack laid there with the problem on his mind, Fawn rolled over toward him and put her arm on his chest. He turned toward her and put his left hand on her waist. This cleared his mind of Barlow. He watched her sleep for a while, then finally dozed off too.

They awoke to the noise, smells and fire lights

that announced a new day in the village. Jack gave Fawn a good-morning kiss. He then left her to finish waking up as he glanced out the open window at the flurry of activity. Besides the usual morning routine of cooking, washing, working and children playing, he saw Chota heading his way. Jack motioned for him to come in and he soon poked his head through the doorway. "When we leave, Jack?"

"Soon," he answered and then looked down at Fawn.

Her eyes lifted to meet his. "Are we leaving?"

"The chief asked me to take the gold in to Tucson and get money for it."

She seemed to be more awake now. "What about Barlow? Aren't you worried someone will see you in town? There's still a price on your head!"

"I've got to deal with Barlow," he said matter-of-factly. "That's why I think you'd better wait here." He knelt beside her.

She then put her arms around his waist. He saw the worry in her eyes. For a long moment, they simply looked at each other.

"It will be fine, I promise. I can take care of myself," he softly assured her. Then his face became stern as his mind flashed to Barlow. "It's time someone took care of Brad Barlow. No one else will do it, and I'm not waiting for a bullet in the back." Then he gave her a smile as he realized he'd raised his voice a little. "Sorry." He kissed her and held her tight.

"I know," she whispered in his ear. "I just thought it wouldn't be so soon."

Two hours later, Jack, Dan and Chota left the boxed canyon. It was a moonlit night. They lead their horses into the rocky gully.

Jack knew what was waiting for him in Tucson. He had faced his share of men before, but this was different. It wasn't just the number he was up against, it was Fawn. His mind kept going back to her lovely face. To that last goodbye. Just as when he had to escape the cavern, he had to put her out of his mind. Yet, not allowing himself to think of the woman that he loved was not easy. Not even for a man like Jack McCall. But this time his life, and that of Dan and Chota, depended on it.

There was a long ride across the desert ahead. Time enough to discipline his mind and to focus on the enemy, Brad Barlow.

Chapter Twelve
Settling Accounts

Traveling to and from his village by night was the usual procedure for Chota. In this way, there was little risk of leading anyone to the village entrance. Walking the horses down the gully for miles was just additional caution. Jack and Dan didn't mind, they understood his dedication to secrecy.

This was Chota's country and he was quite experienced at negotiating the terrain with minimal light. Jack and Dan were happy to simply follow.

It was a quiet and windless night. The air was cool and dry. The moon was in the west, above the distant mountains. The moon's light angled down across the desert floor. It caused a ghostly scene of long, faint shadows.

Jack was glad to be back in open country. He rode along looking up at the stars and taking in the aromas of desert foliage. His cuts, bruises, and strained muscles were largely healed and he felt pretty good. It was time to do a little practice with his guns, to hone his skills.

Just as he had most of his life, he started going through his regiment of drills. No matter what direction he needed to aim, whether standing or on horseback, he had to be equally proficient.

The moon rose higher in the night sky. Chota continued to lead them, mile after mile.

After Jack finished the normal drills, he tried something different. He would look for an object in the distance and pretend it was an adversary. Then he'd draw down on it. He wouldn't shoot, it was just a mock battle. All the same, it was good practice. When he became satisfied that he was back to his usual fast, loose and agile self again, he relaxed. It was a long way into Tucson. Jack would still do the occasional lightening draw from time to time, but he already knew that he was ready.

The three men did little talking as they rode. Perhaps it was crossing the desert by night. Maybe it was the thought of the hired guns in Tucson. Whatever the reason, it made the journey go by slowly. Finally, with about four hours before daybreak, Chota led them to a watering hole. The horses were tired and so were they. Down a rocky wash, where it made an abrupt left bend, was a spring-fed pool. After watering the horses, they tied off their mounts to a mesquite and bunked down for a while.

They awoke to the morning sun. After some dried venison meat and tortillas, courtesy of the chief, they were on their way again. It was mid-morning when they rode into Tucson.

The town was busy. It was something Jack had expected. It was also something that made him very tense. So many people in all directions. There were men on horseback, some were walking along store fronts, still others were coming out of or going into various buildings. Too many to keep track of. Worst of all, he only knew some of Barlow's men by sight. Jack didn't recognize anyone in town from that previous encounter in front of the saloon. Yet, this gave him little comfort. As far as he was concerned, the threat was everywhere and he watched intently for any false move.

Dan led them to the assay office, which was across the street from the bank. They tied their horses to the hitching post in front and stepped up toward the door. Jack felt better getting out of the street. At least he was now able to put his back to the building and could see what, if anything, was coming. While his eyes continued to watch for trouble, he smiled at his friends.

"Can you two stay out of harm's way while I do some business in here?"

"You don't want us to tag along with you, Jack?" Dan seemed puzzled.

"Gold has a way of attracting men who want to know where you got it. I'd just as soon not let anyone know you two are connected with the gold or me."

"What about you, Jack? You not want more men after you?" Chota asked.

"Better me than you two." Jack shrugged. "Besides, I plan on using some intimidation inside. I don't think it will go any further."

Dan nodded. "Okay partner, I guess you know what you're doing. I'll just take Chota with me down to the barbershop. I got a friend there that'll fill me in on what's happened around here since we've been gone."

"You two be careful."

"They ain't after us, Jack," Dan laughed. "The farther away from you, the safer we'll be."

Jack knew there was some truth in what Dan said. He nodded and added, "Meet me in the bank when you're finished at the barbershop."

They both gave a nod and headed down the street. He watched them walk past about twelve stores and then walk inside a building with the standard red and white spiraled post in front. Then Jack went into the assay office.

The assay office was small. On the left side was a counter. It started at the wall by the front door and went nearly to the far wall. A small space at that point allowed entry behind the counter. On the counter were three different sized glass-cased scales, a few bins, and a magnifying glass. Behind the counter was a desk with four levels of shelves above it. On the shelves and scattered on the desk, were the numerous vials and instruments that make up the assayer's laboratory. Sitting at the desk, facing away from Jack was the assayer.

As Jack closed the door behind him, the assayer spun around in his oak swivel chair. "Yes, sir. How can I help you?" He was a thin man in his late thirties with a high monotone voice.

Jack stepped forward, retrieved the gold nugget from his pants pocket, and laid it on the counter. "What's it worth?" he asked without expression.

The assayer's jaw seemed to drop a bit as he stood up. It was only a step to reach the counter. He picked up the nugget with his left hand and stared at it for nearly half a minute. There was a four inch magnifying glass on the counter, to the man's right. He picked it up and studied the gold more closely. "Where'd you get this?" he asked without giving Jack a glance.

"Does it matter?"

"Well, I haven't seen or heard of ore this rich anywhere around here." He looked straight at Jack. "Mister, this is as rich as it gets. Pure gold."

"Good. So what's it worth?"

The assayer could see that he wasn't going to get

much information out of this tough-looking man before him. He opened the glass door as he placed the nugget on the scale. After sliding the weight to the balance point, he noted the reading. Then he went to his desk and did a little figuring with paper and pencil.

He went back to Jack at the counter, paper in hand. "Eighty seven dollars and thirty cents." He held the paper so Jack could see it. "Now, if you give me your name and claim number, I'll make you out a certificate. Then you can go across the street to the bank and get your money."

"Why don't you give me eighty dollars for it? Then you can just forget about the certificate and that I ever even came in here."

The assayer looked Jack over for a moment, then his eyes moved back to the nugget, which was still on the scale. He gave a little smile, turned back to Jack, and nodded. "Alright mister, you've got a deal!" He knelt down behind the counter to, what Jack guessed, was a cash box or small safe. Within a minute, he was standing again and counting out eighty dollars. He handed Jack the money and they shook hands.

Jack McCall was a straight shooter with a gun or words. However, he didn't mind stretching the truth if it meant he could avoid being bushwhacked. He had to be sure this man never told a soul about that gold nugget.

As Jack slid the money into the inside pocket of his vest, he casually said, "You know you're the only person who knows I ever had that nugget."

"Don't worry mister, I won't tell anyone about it." He seemed sincere enough.

Jack smiled, "I know you won't. You're an honest man and we just made a deal." Then the smile vanished. "But, if you ever do," in that instant, the barrel of Jack's right hand .45 suddenly pressed against the assayer's nose, "I'll kill you!" His words were as cold and hard as the barrel of the gun.

Jack spun the Colt back into the holster. He turned and left without another word, leaving the terrified assayer with much to think about.

The town was just as busy as earlier. Leaving the assay office, Jack's eyes swept from side-to-side. He dashed across the street and entered the Bank of Tucson. He was relieved to learn that the bank accepted accounts from Indians. In fact, since the mining boom, banks knew that anyone might have large amounts of money to deposit. It would be poor business to turn them away. So, it was a simple matter of filling out a couple of forms.

While Jack and the bank clerk were doing this, Dan and Chota joined them. All was explained to Chota. He made his mark and was given his bank book.

With business concluded, they moved into the lobby. Before reaching the door, Dan laid his hand on Jack's shoulder. "I've got some bad news, partner. Barlow's promised an extra hundred dollars to his men for killing you." Dan gave Jack a worried look, and then continued. "And my friend at the barbershop saw a couple of Barlow's men coming out of the dry goods store down the street this morning."

"Maybe I ought to ride out first and we'll meet up later, Dan."

"Nope, Chota and me talked about that. We stick together."

"Alright, but there's no point in waiting for more of Barlow's men to show up. Let's go for our horses and get out of here."

Chapter Thirteen
Gunplay

Jack slowly opened the door, put his head out far enough to get a clear view. He then made a scan in all directions. He saw nothing out of the ordinary and turned back to Dan. "Take a look out here, Dakota, you know the Triple B boys by sight, better than I do."

Dan came forward and surveyed the area out front just as Jack did. "I don't see any of Barlow's men either, Jack," he stated this while looking from side-to-side. He then glanced back over his left shoulder. "Maybe we ought to get, while the get-tin's good, partner."

Jack nodded. "Alright, Dan, but let's not waste any time getting to those horses." He looked back at Chota, who gave a nod that he was ready.

Dan pushed the door aside and all three bolted through the doorway.

They managed only a couple steps before Jack saw, from the corner of his eye, two figures rushing out of a doorway from the third building down to his right. As Jack spun to his right, he saw a third man. This man was reaching around the doorway. Jack could see he had a gun in his hand as did the others. Four shots rang out in an instant. Three of them came from Jack's Colts. For the next moment, Jack's guns and eyes stayed fixed in the bushwhacker's direction. Two men were down and not moving. Jack couldn't see the third one. He was, however, pretty certain that he got a piece of him.

He was about to investigate, when he heard a moan to his left. As Jack momentarily turned, he saw Dan holding his right thigh. Blood was seeping through his fingers. Jack had to keep his attention on where the danger was, still, he stepped back a couple feet so he could check on Dan. "How bad is it, Dakota?"

Dan was looking down at his bloody leg, as was Chota. Jack was now right behind them. Dan lifted his hands for a little look-see. He gritted his teeth. "It ain't so bad, Jack. I've been shot a lot worse than this."

Chota looked at Dan quizzically, "You really shot before?"

"Yeah, a few times, but that was a lot of years

ago." Then Dan glanced around at Jack. "Can't say that I missed it much."

That brought a brief smile to Jack's face. Then he put his left hand on Dan's shoulder. "That bullet was intended for me. I'm sorry, Dan."

"Nobody's fault, except Barlow and those no-good hired guns. Now don't worry about me, Jack." Dan motioned toward the two men lying in front of the doorway. "Maybe you could go down there and make sure there ain't anybody left to shoot at us."

Jack turned to Chota. "Help him into the bank and try to stop the bleeding. I'll go down and take a look."

From the second of the shots being fired, the locals scattered. There were people peering out from inside buildings and between them. No one, though, felt safe enough to come out yet. Of course, it had only been maybe a minute or so. It seemed much longer than that.

Jack made his way toward the gunmen's building. It was the third store down. He stayed close to the storefronts so as to be a difficult target. When he reached the suspect building, he saw it was a cobbler's store. It had a large window before the doorway. There was bold white lettering on the glass. It read, WILSON'S SHOE AND BOOT REPAIR.

Jack pulled out his right pistol and held it just below his chin as he carefully took a quick look. There were shelves, displaying assorted footwear behind the window, but it didn't obstruct his field of view.

Jack studied the store's interior more closely through the right edge of the window. His gun and eyes moved as one. The store was clearly unoccupied, but he saw a trail of spattered blood leading to a back door.

The immediate danger now seemed over. Jack walked down for a better look at his fallen enemies. Of course, he knew who they were. In that moment, when he had to draw on them, he recognized their faces from the Longhorn Saloon. He also would have bet that he knew the name of the one that got away.

Jack knelt down and put two fingers against the throats of Les and Cord. It was a mere formality. They were both shot right through the heart. They were probably dead before they hit the boardwalk. Still, he stayed and briefly stared at their faces.

It wasn't remorse that Jack felt. They gave him no choice in the matter. It wasn't pity either. Their lives ended early, but they clearly had it coming. They needed to be killed before they killed others. The thing that Jack felt was anger. He was angry that these men would kill for money. He was angry because these men forced him to kill them.

Killing, even men like these, was a grim business. It wasn't anything new for Jack McCall, but he never got used to it.

After less than a minute, Jack stood up and went into the cobbler's store. He went to the back door. He stood to the right side of the door, turned the handle and pushed it open with his left hand. It was just a precaution, in case Curly McBride was waiting for him. All that Jack saw out back were Les and Cord's horses tied to a hitching post. It seemed plain enough that Curly was on his horse and riding back to the ranch.

By the time Jack rejoined Dan and Chota at the bank, people were starting to emerge from cover. Gunplay wasn't unusual in Tucson. When the shooting stopped, people got on with what they were doing. Jack knew it wouldn't be long before someone went for the marshal.

Using Dan's neckerchief as a dressing and his own belt to complete the bandage, Chota had patched up Dan's wound.

Jack looked at Chota's work and gave him an approving nod.

All three made their way out onto the boardwalk. The town people were now moving pretty freely and one of them was looking at the two dead men.

Dan glanced that direction and then turned to Jack, "So, did you recognize those two hombres?"

"Les and Cord," Jack stated flatly. "Pretty sure Curly McBride was the other one."

"Figures, those three always ran together."

"I'm afraid McBride got away. I winged him, but he's probably halfway to the ranch by now."

"That's bad, Jack! They'll bring a whole army in here to get you."

"No doubt. It's just a matter of how long before they get here."

"I got an idea, Jack." Despite the pain, Dan managed a little smile.

"I'll listen to anything, Dan, but don't you think I better square myself with the marshal now?"

"Bad idea, partner. That marshal is bought and paid for, and Barlow's holding the bill of sale."

"Then we're just wasting time here, Dakota."

Dan put an arm on Jack and Chota's shoulders. They headed across the street to the horses. "You two help me up on my pony, then follow me. I've got a plan."

Chapter Fourteen
Dan's Plan

The Triple B was about twelve miles from town. Even if Curly McBride pushed his horse the whole way to the ranch, Jack and company had some time. Barlow would have to round up his men and then send them into town. Dan knew this and he knew which way they'd be coming. The trail the Triple B boys would be taking followed the railroad from town for seven miles. It then turned southeast for another five miles to the ranch.

Dan explained what he had in mind as he led them along the railroad route. The trail that Dan took was north of the tracks. Barlow's men would be traveling a parallel path, but several miles to the south. Dan's plan was to stay out of their sight by taking the long way around, knowing Barlow's boys would take the direct route. At the point where the trail to the ranch turned southeast, there were a series of hills. They overlooked the trail.

Jack and Chota followed Dan as he took them to the top of the most prominent hilltop. They tied their horses behind some large rocks. Jack and Chota then helped Dan off his horse. They found a suitable observation point, sat down amongst some brush, and waited.

There was no sign of dust yet. They had a commanding view of the rolling landscape. Jack's eyes took it all in with one sweep. It was mostly scrub grass, punctuated with brush and the occasional rocks; the cactus were in patches. Off to the left was a meandering line of small trees. A wash or creek bed, he figured.

Jack looked down at Dan's wound. All the traveling and movement had gotten it bleeding again. "We've got to get your leg tended to, Dan."

"I don't fancy goin' back into town right now, Jack. I'd rather bleed a little than let Barlow's men get a hold of me."

Chota reached down, adjusted the neckerchief a bit and tightened the belt. "I can take him to Papago village, they fix Dan good."

"That's fine, Chota, but we gotta help Jack here first." Dan then turned to Jack and gave a firm nod.

"I appreciate you being willing to go into harm's way with me partners." Jack glanced out across the desert. "But, all I really need is the lay of that ranch." He looked back at Dakota Dan. "I guess you know this place."

"Sure do, Jack. I used to go there when it belonged to Swede Svenson. We used to go huntin' together."

"How should I approach the place?"

Dan pointed to his left. "You see that line of trees out yonder?"

Jack nodded.

"That's a fair-sized creek, comes out of the Sierra Colorado Mountains. Anyway, it's deep enough to hide a man if he were to ride down in it." Dan then pointed a little to the right. "Now, see that little hill in the distance?"

Jack gave another nod.

"That creek goes right by the foot of that hill. You won't be able to see it then, but you'll be real close to the ranch. Tie up your pony and then climb up and take a peek. You'll want to pick a spot where the barn comes between you and the bunkhouse to make your move. From there, you should be able to mosey up without bein' seen."

"And how are the buildings laid out?"

"Well, first, there's a corral between the creek and the barn. Then comes the bunkhouse, not too far beyond it. But then it's a fair ways to the main house."

"And Barlow."

"And more gun hands. You can count on that!"

"No doubt, but you've been a big help Dan, Thanks!"

"But no telling how many men will be around, Jack. How you gonna do it?"

"I'll figure out something. But if Barlow sends most of his men into town, like we think, that should narrow the odds."

"And you'll have, like they say in the army, the element of surprise."

"Yeah, I think I can give them a few surprises." Jack smiled at his friends.

"Well, it don't seem right, us letting you go up against all those men alone, partner."

"Don't worry about me, Dan. I just need to find a way to deal with Barlow. The Triple B is like a snake and Barlow's the snake's head."

"I don't get you, Jack," he wore a puzzled look.

"Don't matter how long the snake, cut off the head and you can forget about the rest of it."

Dan nodded, "I see what you mean, Jack." He then pointed out across the desert. "I think I see a whole lot of snake coming this way."

In the distance was a growing dust cloud. All three watched it come toward them and finally turn toward the railroad tracks. When it made the turn, Jack tried to judge the number of riders. From that distance it was hard to tell, but he guessed thirty.

As Barlow's army moved on, Jack and Chota

helped Dan back to his horse. They then got him on board. Dan looked down at Jack and gave a little sigh. "Good luck, partner!"

"Thanks, Dan. Take care of that leg."

Jack and Chota simply exchanged nods.

Just as they started to turn their horses to leave, Dan looked back at Jack. "It's been really something riding with you."

"Has it been interesting, Dan?"

Dakota Dan gave half a smile and a terse shake of the head. "Mighty, Jack, mighty!"

He rode away without looking back.

Chapter Fifteen
Element of Surprise

There was no way of knowing how much time Jack had. He knew that Barlow's army was going into town. How long they'd linger there without finding their quarry was hard to figure. Jack wouldn't waste time. He mounted Chilco, headed down the hill and then made for the creek at a gallop. It wasn't long before he reached the dry creek and found a bank with a gradual incline in which to enter.

Just as Dan had told him, the creek was deep enough to hide a rider. Winter storms and flash floods had done their work over the years to carve a small canyon. It wandered and varied in size.

Jack remembered the two miners that he and Dan had located by the dust that they stirred up in the wash. He didn't make the same mistake. Jack kept the speed down.

After several miles, Jack saw a hill up to his left. Following Dan's instructions, he dismounted and tied Chilco to a bush. It wasn't possible to climb the bank in many places. Where erosion had caused the creek wall to tumble down, Jack climbed up and viewed the ranch.

The barn was dark red and quite large. Behind it was a smaller building, also red, obviously the bunkhouse with a cookhouse attached. Then, behind that was the ranchhouse. It was a large one-story, mid-western style place. There were a few steps leading up to a couple of wooden pillars. After that was a small porch and then the wide entry door. The house was white and trimmed with pale green.

Jack could see no one outside at the moment. He did, however, notice horses tied in front of the main house. There were more in front of the bunkhouse. From his angle, he couldn't tell how many.

Jack climbed back down the bank. He untied Chilco and led him along until the barn would shield his approach from any ranchhands. He found another section of bank which he could scale, retied Chilco to a heavy rock, and made his ascent.

After a brief scan to see if anyone was around, Jack simply walked toward the barn. There was a small corral attached to the back of the barn where

Jack was headed. It was empty, so he ducked between the wooden rails and continued to the rear barn door. He paused to listen at the door. Satisfied that there were only animal sounds within, he carefully opened the door. All that could be seen were a few horses, cows, and a lot of hay. He passed through the interior of the barn and stopped again at the large double front doors. Jack then opened the doors just far enough that he could see what was ahead.

Jack was looking at the side of the cookhouse. Behind it, attached, was the bunkhouse. There were five horses in front to Jack's left. The horse on the end, closest to Jack, was dripping with sweat.

The bunkhouse was a long building. The cookhouse was smaller. It looked like it had been added, Jack guessed, as the ranch grew. Smoke was coming from the metal chimney. The smell of beans, tortillas, and beef filled the air. The sound of voices could be heard from the bunkhouse. There were only a couple of small, stark windows at the front side of the cookhouse. There were two larger windows with white curtains at the back.

Jack slipped through the barn doors and went to the back of the cookhouse. He peeked inside. It was a cramped little home, the cook's quarters. That made sense, it seemed to Jack, cooks have to be up earlier than the ranchhands, so they live behind the kitchen. Jack walked over to the first little kitchen window and looked in. There at the stove was a middle-aged and rather round Mexican man. Behind him, working on some tortillas on the counter facing the other way, was an equally round Mexican woman. *Husband and wife*, Jack thought.

He then saw that there was a front door and a door also on the far wall that opened into the bunkhouse.

Jack made the corner to enter the kitchen. He quietly opened the door and casually walked up to the male cook. He approached with one finger over his mouth. As the man turned and looked his way, Jack moved his finger from his lips and softly spoke, "Habla quedito por favor."

"I speak English, señor," he answered in a soft tone.

Jack moved closer so he could speak at a whisper. "There's going to be some trouble, amigo. Could you and your wife go into your room and stay very quiet? I don't want you two hurt."

The man seemed to study Jack from head to toe, "You're the man Señor Barlow wants killed, aren't you?" He kept his voice at a whisper, too.

Jack gave a nod.

"All those men after one man," he shook his head. "It's not fair. It's not right."

"I don't think Barlow's very interested in fair or right."

"Señor Barlow is a hard man. Just a week ago, he

told my wife the coffee was too hot and slapped her."

Jack looked her way and she lowered her head.

"We only stay here because we are afraid to leave." He then went to his wife, put his hand on her shoulder, and started escorting her to their room. As he closed the door behind him, he paused and looked back at Jack. "Good luck, señor."

Jack started looking around at all the food. He was hungry. He poured a cup of coffee, spooned some meat and beans onto a plate and leaned back against a countertop.

As Jack downed his lunch, he listened to the voices in the bunkhouse. Through the chatter, he heard five different voices. One was a familiar voice, and it was no surprise. He knew that the over-heated and sweat drenched horse outside had to belong to Curly McBride.

Although he hadn't heard the beginning of the conversation next door, he did hear the part where Curly thought that he was entitled to at least some of the bounty. In Curly's version, he had stood up to Jack. The others in the room were suitably impressed.

Jack was less impressed. He had no use for a bushwhacker and was plenty mad about Dan being shot. He took one last mouthful of pinto beans and meat. Then he pushed the bunkhouse door open and walked in like he owned the place.

Jack immediately sized up the situation. The bunks were arranged side-by-side and up against both walls. There was wide walking space between the rows. The place reminded him of a army barracks.

Curly McBride was propped up in a bunk against the far wall, a little to Jack's right and facing him. There was a thick white bandage around his right upper arm. He was covered to the chest with a tan Mexican blanket.

There were four cowpokes near the foot of his bed. They were facing Curly. They now turned toward him. All four carried six-guns. Jack didn't judge them as a particular threat. The four young and dusty men looked at Jack McCall with startled expressions.

Before anyone began to speak, Jack saw the shape of a gun barrel, just to the right of Curly's hip, raising up under Curly's blanket. Without hesitation, and in a blink of an eye, he put one .45 slug into the center of Curly's forehead. As the sound of the blast bounced around the room, and the smell and smoke from the powder still hung in the air, Jack spun the left hand Colt he'd just fired back into its holster.

At that moment, all four men turned their heads

to see Curly expire. They looked back at Jack with confusion and anger.

From their appearance, each wore chaps, spurs, and sweat-stained work shirts and a thick coating of red dust, Jack figured they were just back from the herd. None of them looked to be older than their late twenties.

The pale redhead on the far right wasn't more than nineteen. Next to him was a tall and skinny fellow who was minus a couple of upper teeth. To the left of him was a short and stocky-looking Mexican lad. The last man, who was far left at the foot of Curly's bunk, had to be the oldest. He looked well fed and at least as caught off guard as the others.

In that very still moment, Jack studied the four cowpokes. *They are clearly afraid to look away, but are they afraid to draw?* Jack wondered.

From where Jack stood, he could see either the front or back doors of the bunkhouse with the flick of his eyes. There were small windows on each side of both doors. He could tell if anyone was coming. A good position from a gunfighter's perspective.

After a quick glance at Curly's cold lifeless face, and the trail of blood oozing from the wound, Jack gave the four men an equally cold look.

So far that day, Jack had killed three men, and he hadn't even seen Barlow yet. One way or another, he had to deal with these four. He would just as soon not have to kill them. In fact, he had other plans for them. All the same, if they wanted to fight, he would kill them, and he wanted them to know it.

"In case you boys ain't figured it out already, the name's McCall." His voice seemed to build with anger. "Now I know you Triple B boys want to collect that bounty for me." Jack took a step forward. They were only a few feet apart now, and he stared at each one in turn. "So, maybe you cowboys think you're fast. Or maybe you're thinking there's four of you and just one of me," he looked into each man's eyes. "So, what's it gonna be, boys? One at a time, or all at once? It don't make a bit of difference to me!"

For the next few seconds, it was a silent face-off. Jack knew it could go either way. Although these men were primarily cowpokes, he sensed their blood was up. It wasn't just the money and their pride. Jack had just killed their friend. No matter what kind of man Curly was, he was their friend. The tension was building.

The redhead was moving his fingers and looking like a spring about to snap. The Mexican had a crazy look in his eyes. Jack, on the other hand, looked completely calm and confident. Then, in what could only be described as an anti-climax, the tall skinny one broke the silence with one word, "NO!" He then raised his hands while saying, "He's too fast, he'll kill all of us!"

With those words, whatever resolve the other

three had, disappeared. The anger was still there, but their hands went up.

Jack had excellent peripheral vision, still he looked to each door and window, making sure there were no unwanted guests. He then motioned to the chubby man at the foot of Curly's bunk. "Pull that blanket down a couple feet."

He complied. There, still in Curly McBride's hand was a Remington revolver.

"Reach over and pick up that gun by the barrel."

He did as Jack said and then started to offer it to him.

Jack held up his hand. "No, just take out the cylinder and toss it to me."

He pulled back the rod and the cylinder dropped into his hand, then he made the toss. Jack caught it and slid it into his pocket.

The big cowboy looked down at the pistol and then at Jack. "How'd you know Curly had a gun under that blanket?" he spoke with a slow drawl.

"I saw it pointing up at me from under the blanket. He was about to dry-gulch me for the second time today."

The cowpoke dropped the Remington on the floor and turned toward his friends. They wore surprised expressions. The redheaded boy looked over to Jack. As he spoke, he sounded almost apologetic, "I figured, heck, we all figured, you just shot Curly down, mister!"

Jack stated flatly, "You figured wrong." He wasn't about to show a soft side now. It was important for them to retain a fear of him.

Then, with such blinding speed that it made the four cowboys question their own eyes, Jack drew and aimed his Colts in their direction. "Alright, boys, pull out those pistols and start unloading them!" He made a tilting motion with the left hand .45, "Now, I want to see six bullets in your hands."

As they rotated the cylinders and pushed out the cartridges, Jack glanced from side-to-side to see if he had company. "Is Barlow up at the house?" he asked indifferently.

"Yeah, that's what Curly said," the redhead spoke up, while he retrieved the last bullet and looked up at Jack.

"So, how many men are up there with him?" Jack looked back at the young man.

He shrugged his shoulders, "We spent the morning rounding up strays and just got back a little while ago, so, we don't really know, Mr. McCall. We just heard that he sent a lot of men out to find you, but there's usually at least a couple in there. Mr. Barlow worries a lot about his safe."

Jack felt the young cowhand was being straight with him. He gave him a couple nods and then looked to see that there were six bullets in the four men's hands. "Alright, then, give those bullets a toss." He pointed toward the far end of the bunkhouse with his right pistol.

After they threw them and the pelting and rolling sounds stopped, the chubby man turned to Jack. He showed just a glint of a smile. "If you don't mind me asking, mister, how do you expect to get into that house without getting shot first? It's a long way to that house, and it's all open ground."

"And they know I'm coming," Jack added.

"They had to hear the shot. They're just waiting for you." His smile grew a little. "So, how you gonna do it?"

"It won't be so bad," Jack replied, "because you're going with me."

"Me? No thanks, mister. This is your play." He shook his head.

"You'll do it, and so will you three." Jack glanced at his friends.

They looked at one another and looked at Jack like he was crazy.

"Do what I tell you and you'll be fine. Anything else and you'll be dead." He stated it bluntly and then motioned toward the door with his left revolver.

The four men moved toward the front door of the bunkhouse while showing considerable displeasure. Jack followed them to the door, halting them before opening it with, "Alright, here's how it will go."

They turned around to face Jack.

"When we mosey up to that house, I want two of you on each side of me, and point those empty guns my way like you're tough hombres." He then focused on the chubby man. "You do the talking, but remember, all you're gonna say is, 'We got him, Mr. Barlow.' Then, when we get closer you'll say, 'We're bringing him to you.' Nothing else!"

Jack could see they were scared and wanted no part of it. "Now, you men do this and I'll let you go. But, I mean go. You get on your ponies and ride. Don't come back, or it'll be the last mistake you ever make. Now, there are plenty of other ranches east of here. You've been working for the wrong man long enough." He gave them another hard stare and added. "Don't cross me or you'll be dead before you hit the ground."

They all did a little swallowing and then gave a nod. The chubby man and Red came out first. Jack followed, then as the Mexican and the skinny galute took their place on each side, Jack put his hands and guns behind his back.

As they rounded the bunkhouse, they came into full view of the ranchhouse. Those inside would think that Jack's hands were tied.

Jack could see curtains moving in the windows. Their approach was being watched carefully.

When they reached about the halfway point, Jack

whispered to Chubby, "Tell him. You call it out, just like I said."

After a hesitation, he looked ahead at the house and did a pretty convincing job. "We got him, Mr. Barlow!" he yelled out.

They continued toward the house. Jack's escorts walked a little sideways so they could aim their guns and watch their mock prisoner. With about twenty paces to go before the steps leading up to the porch and front door, Jack whispered again. "Tell him we're coming."

"We're bringing him to you," Chubby announced.

As they approached the stairs, the wide, cedar door opened. A tall and lanky man wearing a plaid shirt, navy pants and his pistol low, stood in the doorway.

Jack and his guards climbed the stairs and stopped momentarily on the porch. The lanky gun-hand stepped back to make way for Jack and his escorts. There was a wry smile beneath his dark mustache. As they entered, he moved back and to his right. He joined another gunman wearing a pale blue shirt with brown suspenders connected to his dungaree pants.

Behind them was a large black safe. On the right side of the large formal room, and standing a little farther back was a third gun-hand.

Jack was struck by him immediately. It wasn't the

knee-length black coat, white silk shirt, or even the expensive-looking gray slacks that got his attention. His low-slung holster and Colt revolver were much like the ones carried by his two compatriots across the room. What made him different was his eyes. Even from a distance, Jack could tell. He was no local gun-hand. He was a gunfighter, or what many called a shootist.

There was a neat order to the room. From the furniture, the rugs on the floor, to the European style paintings on the walls, there was a precision about the place. Even the roll-top desk, at which Brad Barlow was sitting, had all papers, books, blotters, and pens in perfect arrangement.

Jack and his four escorts now stood just inside the orderly room. Barlow, adorned in a gray pin-stripped suit, had been sitting at his desk in a swivel chair, turned halfway around, and watched their arrival. He turned the chair toward Jack and smiled as he stood up. He took a few steps in Jack's direction and stopped just before him.

Savoring the moment, he put his hands on his hips and looked Jack straight in the eyes. A big grin was evident on his face as he spoke. "I'm going to enjoy this!"

Jack's eyebrows raised a bit. "Of all the men I've shot, you're the first one that thought he was gonna enjoy it." Jack couldn't resist a half smile as he brought around his two pistols, pointing the left one at Barlow's nose and the right one toward the shootist.

As terror replaced the grin on Barlow's face, Jack spoke just loud enough for his escorts, "You boys can go now."

They left the room with considerable haste. Jack knew he didn't have to worry about them coming back. Those boys would know that even if Barlow somehow came out of this on top, he would view them as traitors. They'd put as many miles as possible between them and the ranch by nightfall.

Jack kept most of his attention on the two gun-hands to his left and the more serious gunman to his right. With Barlow standing before him, suddenly speechless, the shooter stepped closer. "A man like you doesn't need to shoot an unarmed man. There's no challenge in it." His voice was calm and low. There was something of a swagger in his movement. He was a well-built man with attractive features. In his eyes, you could read cold confidence. Cocky was the word that came to Jack's mind.

"You want to take his place?" Jack asked indifferently.

"Oh, yes," he answered as he came forward and pulled the somewhat petrified Barlow by his shoulder, back out of his way. Getting a hold of himself a little, Barlow then moved over to the other two gun-hands by the safe and out of the line of fire.

Jack glanced over at Barlow and his men at that

moment. His new adversary looked too. "This is private. You two stay out of it!" the shootist stated firmly.

They nodded and Jack spun his Colts back into their holsters.

"I've been waiting for you, McCall. Been looking forward to facing you."

"Really?" Jack answered with disdain. "I can't imagine giving you a thought." He had contempt for hired guns and men who killed for reputation alike. Not surprisingly, his response angered the shootist.

"I guess you don't know who I am."

Jack didn't even change his expression.

Frustration and anger could be seen in the face of a man used to being respected. "The name's Tex Foley."

This also got no reaction from Jack.

"They call me Too Fast Tex, fastest gun in Texas!" He spoke those words with pride.

"Too bad," Jack answered casually.

"What's too bad?"

"Too bad we ain't in Texas."

Hearing that, Foley went for his Colt. The fastest gun in Texas managed to get his gun halfway out of its holster before Jack put one bullet between its owner's eyes. Tex Foley and most of his brain were now spread out on Barlow's otherwise tidy floor.

Jack turned to the remaining gun-hands. "Who's

next?" he twirled the smoking Colt in his right hand and then sunk it back into its holster.

"Not me!" came out of the mouths of both men, nearly at the same time. Whatever courage and confidence they might have had was long gone. Both men moved their hands away from their guns.

Jack walked over to the two gun-hands standing alongside Barlow. All three were about as scared as Jack had ever seen. He wanted to deal with Barlow alone, but prefered running these two off to killing them. If a man's scared enough, Jack figured, they'd do just about anything. "I can't think of one good reason why I shouldn't blow your no-good heads off," Jack stated as he looked them over with disgust.

"Wait a minute, mister," the lanky gun-hand's voice sounded high and desperate. "We just work here, no need for any killing. Heck, you let us go, and you'll never see us again." His partner seemed willing to let him do all the talking.

"What are you two willing to do to save your lousy hides?"

"Anything, mister, you name it." Lanky nodded, as did his partner.

"Toss those gun belts in the corner."

They did.

"Take off those boots."

They looked at each other for a moment, then complied.

"The pants."

"I heard about you doing this to other men." There was just a trace of defiance in Lanky's tone.

"You've got a choice." Jack's eyes moved over to the gun belts in the corner.

Lanky looked at Jack and then reached down for his belt buckle. "Ain't no pants worth dying for."

They both now stood in their red longjohns. Their trousers lay in a heap on the floor by their feet and boots.

"Now, grab those boots and take a walk, no horses."

As they slid their feet back into their boots, Jack pointed in the direction of the road to town. "That's where you're going, Tucson. Now what's gonna happen if you do anything else?"

Lanky looked over his shoulder while heading for the door, "You'll kill us?"

"Count on it!" Jack then watched out the window long enough to see them walk through the gate and head for town.

He then turned to Barlow, who stood alone and afraid. "You haven't said much, Mr. Barlow." Jack made a quick survey of his enemy's condition. He was a pathetic sight. There was a trickle of tears from both eyes. He was having trouble swallowing. His hands were trembling. Barlow took a breath and looked back at Jack. "What do you want me to say?" His voice quivered.

"How about goodbye?" Jack stated flatly, while he pulled his right hand Colt out and pointed it at Barlow's forehead.

As Barlow heard the *click, click* sound of Jack cocking the gun, he began to plead. He closed his eyes and repeated, "Don't kill me, Mr. McCall. Please don't kill me!"

"Give me one good reason, Barlow."

"Money!" he looked up at Jack. "I have money. You take it. Take it all!" his voice was frantic.

"You better not be lying Barlow. Show me and I mean now!"

Barlow scurried over to his safe and started going through the combination.

Jack didn't show it, but he was amused at Barlow being so predictable. Brad Barlow couldn't know that Jack would never shoot an unarmed man, or the bluff wouldn't have worked. One way or the other, he planned to coerce him into opening that safe. Somehow, it seemed better that Barlow volunteered.

In spite of his jittery hands, he got the right numbers and the safe's door opened. Jack stood behind him and noticed that Barlow's obsession with order carried on within the safe. All items inside were stacked, aligned, and arranged for tidy order.

"Alright, Barlow, bring out the cash and also the deeds to all your property, too."

He carefully gathered a stack of one inch high

bundles of bills and picked up a manila envelope, labeled DEEDS.

"Stand over by your desk and face me."

Barlow did as he was told. Jack then checked through the safe while keeping an eye on Barlow at the same time. There was everything from tax records to payroll accounts, but nothing else of interest to Jack.

He walked over to Barlow. "Put everything on your desk. Have a seat and grab a pen."

Barlow stacked the six bundles of banded bills on the left side of the desk. He placed the envelope in the center. His writing equipment was already on the right hand side. He sat down in the swivel chair, turned and faced the desk.

Jack reached down over Barlow's left shoulder, with his left hand, to pick up one of the bundles of money. As he did so, Barlow seemed to be settling into the chair to write. What Jack didn't know was that Barlow kept a loaded .45 snapped into place on the underside of that desk. As he examined the money, Barlow was slipping his right hand beneath the desktop. Jack's attention was on the brown paper band that was wrapped around the bills when Barlow made his move.

Suddenly, he spun left in his chair while swinging the gun around by his left shoulder. Just as the gun barrel was coming around to point blank range, Jack simply snatched it out of Barlow's hand.

Briefly, Jack just held the gun in his right hand and looked at Barlow's shattered expression. He tossed it a couple of feet into the air, causing it to spin, and caught it by the handle. He twirled it back and forth, as though he was checking the feel and balance. Then he glanced down at the Colt and back at Barlow. "Thanks, but I don't really need another gun." He said it casually, as he threw it over with the gun-hands hardware. "Now, sign the deeds, Barlow!"

There was no more defiance in Brad Barlow. He pulled the deeds of the ranches he'd taken by force and intimidation out of the large envelope and started signing the releases.

Jack looked on for maybe a minute and then stated, "You like things to be real neat and orderly don't you?"

He gave a couple nods.

"So, where'd you get into that habit?"

After a brief hesitation, he sighed, "I, well, I used to be an accountant."

"For the Bureau of Indian Affairs?"

Barlow snapped his head around. "How'd you know that?"

Jack held the bundle of bills before his eyes. On the brown paper band were printed those words.

Barlow closed his eyes and grimaced.

Jack wondered if Barlow left those bands around that money because he liked things neat, or if it was some sort of reminder of how far he'd come. Maybe both with a bit of arrogance thrown in.

Jack decided to throw some conjecture Barlow's way and see what sort of reaction he got. "So, I suppose you worked as a dutiful employee, but all the time you were planning this. When enough money was there, and you had your chance, you grabbed it and jumped on the first train west. Then you got to live your dream of being a cattle baron."

Jack was just guessing and Barlow wasn't talking. Still, judging from Barlow's expression, it was pretty close.

Jack motioned for Barlow to finish up with the deeds. Before long, he had signed the last one. Jack then gathered up the money and deeds and he tucked them into various pockets on his person. "Come on Barlow, let's go."

"Where?" His reaction was surprise.

"We're going for a ride."

"Come on Mr. McCall," Barlow seemed tired and utterly defeated. "You've taken everything I have. There's nothing left."

"What I took, you stole in the first place, Barlow. But you still have your life. If you want to keep it, you'll do what I say."

Barlow, dejectedly, started moving toward the door. Jack went over and picked up the trousers left by the gun-hands and draped them over his left shoulder. He hoped presenting them to Dan would bring a smile and make him feel better.

Jack then followed Barlow out the door. Barlow started to go to his horse, but Jack nudged him on. Jack knew better than to use Barlow's horse. He didn't want to give anyone a trail to follow.

When they got into the barn, Jack had Barlow saddle one of the horses in there. With Barlow leading the horse, they then headed out the back door of the barn and into the back corral. On the right side of the corral was a gate. Once through the gate, Jack directed his captive toward the creek. The horse, quite naturally balked at descending the rugged bank into the creek. It took several minutes to coax and pull him down.

After Jack put the money, deeds, and britches into his saddlebags, they mounted and rode off.

Chapter Sixteen
No Chances

It was a very quiet ride. Barlow made attempts to find out where he was being taken, but Jack did not respond. Jack had a couple reasons for giving Barlow the silent treatment. One, was that he thought not knowing would be more agonizing than if he actually knew. Second, was that Jack had no use for Barlow and he simply didn't want to talk to him.

The route started as a basic backtrack of how he had gone to the ranch. However, they stayed in the creek until they were well north of the railroad tracks. It was Jack's intention to give Barlow's little army and Tucson itself, a wide berth. When they began riding west, the tracks and Tucson were miles to the south. It would be a long ride this way, but Jack saw no point in taking chances now.

It took the rest of the day, still, they safely skirted Tucson and headed for the Papago village. It was nearly dark when they arrived at Mission San Xavier.

Jack's arrival caused some commotion. It wasn't necessary for Jack to seek out Chota. He had gotten the word and came over to greet him. It didn't take long to explain the circumstance with Barlow. Chota then sent for one of the tribe's council members.

Upon hearing what Barlow had done, he was more than willing to hold him in custody. The Indian agent was due in about a week and a half. He made regular rounds of the various nearby reservations and could be counted on to show up about the same time each month. Since he was an official representative of the United States to the Indian Nations, he would have special interest in Barlow. The tribe arranged a round-the-clock guard of him until then.

With Barlow taken off his hands, Jack wanted to see Dan. Chota pointed out the hut where he was convalescing. He told Jack he'd meet him there after he found him some food. Jack went to his horse, pulled off the saddlebags, and headed for Dan's hut.

Jack ducked down to clear the low door opening.

There was a little fire going in the center of the hut. Around the simple hearth, lay woven grass mats that covered the entire floor. There were baskets and clay pots against the far wall. Cooking utensils lay just left of the fire. On the other side of the fire resting on several brightly colored blankets was Dakota Dan.

A big grin lit up his face as Jack came in and sat beside him. "It's mighty good to see you, partner!" He said that as he scooted up on the rolled white blanket his head had been resting on.

"It's good to see you too, amigo. How's the leg?"

"Well, they sent some big Indian gal in here to dig out the slug. That weren't no fun at all. But she patched me up pretty good. I'm gonna be just fine." He then wiggled and pushed so he was sitting up straight. "So, tell me Jack. What happened at that ranch?"

"Well, first thing, Dan, I owe you one. It wouldn't have been so easy if you didn't show me how to slip in the back door."

Dan smiled, "So, you got the drop on them?"

"Pretty much, but two of them wanted to fight. I had to kill Curly McBride and an hombre named Tex Foley."

Dan's eyebrows raised a little, "I thought Foley was one fast man with a gun!"

"So did he," Jack said matter-of-factly and opened his saddlebag. "I managed to run off the other six." Jack then retrieved the two trousers and handed them to Dan. "A couple of them ended up walking into town without these. Thought you might like to add them to your collection."

Dan's eyes seemed to sparkle, "Wish I could have been there to see it, partner. That must have been something!"

"You think you would have found it interesting?"

"Mighty, partner."

Jack gave a little smile, "I have a couple of favors to ask, Dan."

"Name them. Anything, Jack."

He reached in his saddlebag, brought out the six bundles of bills and passed them to Dan. "All that money that Barlow came here with and used to buy up ranches, was stolen from the Bureau of Indian Affairs. Seems he worked there as an accountant. Now in about ten days or so, the Indian agent will be coming here. So, if you're up to it, you can give him the money and fill him in. Then that Indian agent can take Barlow and turn him over to a Federal Marshal."

"Sure, Jack, I'll just need some rest. I'll be up and about by then. What else?"

Jack took out the deeds and handed them to Dan. "Barlow was nice enough to sign these over," Jack smiled. "If you could find out where the folks are that he fleeced out of their property, you can send these to them."

Dan nodded, "I got a friend that works at the post office. We'll get these to their rightful owners."

Just as Jack put his hand on Dan's shoulder and gave him a grateful nod, Chota came in. He went to Jack with a shallow basket of food. He handed him the basket, "I have boy feed and water your horse. You eat now."

Jack gave a little smile. "Thanks, Chota." He went through the beans, tortillas, and corn without speaking. He then stood up and looked at his two friends. "I've got to go," he said with some impatience.

"I reckon I understand, partner." Dan held out a hand.

Chota simply nodded.

Jack shook both men's hands and quickly left. He mounted Chilco and headed out into the desert.

Chapter Seventeen
Night Ride

Jack rode all night. When the glow of the sun first began to spread across the sandy plain, he had reached the rocky gully. As before, he dismounted and lead his horse within the gully, following Chota's precautions. Soon he was at the canyon below the two spires.

As he walked Chilco into the canyon leading to the hidden city, he was amused by his own behavior. This wasn't like him, riding across the desert, through the darkness, while desperately tired.

Dan and Chota knew why, with no words spoken. They knew what compelled Jack and it wasn't the city beneath the sand. It was Fawn.

Once at the entrance, he rolled the stone door open, lead Chilco inside and rolled the stone back in place. He wasted little time stabling his horse and was soon through the second stone doorway. As he descended the first ladder, he noticed how quiet it was below. It was also nearly dark. The last of the fires were being extinguished and the city was going to sleep.

Jack made his way down to the courtyard without being noticed. There were a couple of women by the fountain that turned his way as he passed, but he put his finger over his lips. They smiled and said nothing. He continued on until he reached the bottom level room that the chief had let them use. Quietly, he went to the doorway and peered inside. She was there, sleeping sweetly upon a thick mat at the far side of the room. A folded blanket was beneath her head, she was facing his way.

Momentarily, he just stood there watching her in the dim light, barely able to make out the features of her lovely face in the shadowy darkness. He silently crossed the room and knelt beside her, then bent down and gently kissed her on the cheek. As her eyes opened and she realized that it wasn't just a dream, her face seemed to light up. Jack looked into her eyes and ran a finger through her hair. "I missed you."

She put her arms around his neck, pulled him down to her and gave him a long kiss. Then, as her senses cleared of the last mist of sleep, the thought of Barlow and his men flashed across her mind. She pushed him back a little and looked him straight in the eyes. “Is everything alright?”

Jack smiled, “It is now.”

Decent
2/8/06 Nothing special, but a good story. R.D.

Good Book Really enjoyed it.